TALES OF THE WHITE MOUNTAINS

Hawthorne at thirty-six. Portrait by Charles Osgood, 1840.

Tales of the White Mountains

by Nathaniel Hawthorne

Introduction and Historical Epilogue
"The Willey Slide Disaster and
Mountain Culture"
by John T. B. Mudge

THE DURAND PRESS
ETNA, NEW HAMPSHIRE

Printed in the United States of America.

Imprint is last number shown: 9 8 7 6 5 4 3 2 1

ISBN 0-9708324-0-0

Cover and text design by May10 Design, West Lebanon, NH.
The text of this book is set in Stempel Garamond.

Unless noted below, all illustrations are courtesy of the
Durand Press. The illustration on page II is courtesy of the
Peabody Essex Museum in Salem, Massachusetts. The
photograph on page X is courtesy of the National Archives.
The illustrations on pages 100 and 128 are courtesy of the
New Hampshire Historical Society. The illustrations on pages
7, 86, 108, 109, and 123 are courtesy of the Dartmouth
College Library, Rauner Special Collections. The Howe
Library of Hanover, New Hampshire, the New York Public
Library, and the Boston Public Library provided assistance is
locating some of the old newspapers that are quoted in the
epilogue. The assistance of all of these institutions is greatly
appreciated.

Cover illustration: *Mount Washington, and the White Hills,
(From near Crawford's)* by William H. Bartlett for *American
Scenery*, London 1838–1839. Bartlett's drawings of the White
Mountains, though greatly romanticized and exaggerated, were
based on observations that he made when he visited New
Hampshire. Published in London, these drawings contributed
to the international popularity of the White Mountains.
Though some of Bartlett's fellow artists criticized his work,
others took advantage of its popularity by copying it in their
paintings. Some of those artists never visited New Hampshire.
Other prints by Bartlett are reprinted on pages 12 and 91.

TABLE OF CONTENTS

Introduction

NATHANIEL HAWTHORNE, a shy, quiet, and reclusive individual, was one of America's greatest writers. During his lifetime he was described as having "bold imagination," "quiet humor," "a fine tone of sadness," and "elegance of style." Henry Wadsorth Longfellow wrote that Hawthorne's writings "comes from the hand of a genius." He is best remembered for two works, *The House of Seven Gables* and *The Scarlet Letter*. However, he also wrote four pieces about the White Mountains of New Hampshire that are an important part of the literary history of that region and which introduced many people elsewhere to the White Mountains.

Nathaniel Hawthorne was born in Salem, Massachusetts, on July 4, 1804. Hawthorne's father, Nathaniel Hathorne, was a sea caption who died of yellow fever in Dutch Guiana, now Suriname, when Nathaniel was a small child. Nathaniel added the "w" to the family name. One of Hawthorne's ancestors, William Hathorne, who had come to America in 1630, had ordered the whipping of a Quaker woman in Colonial Massachusetts. William's son, John Hathorne, was one of the judges at the Salem Witch Trials. After the death of Hawthorne's father the family lived with his mother's family, the Mannings. In 1816, the family moved to Raymond, Maine, near Sebago Lake, to a farm owned by the Manning family. After spending three years in Maine, where Hawthorne explored the surrounding woods and hills, the family returned to Salem where he finished school. Hawthorne then attended Bowdoin College, then a college of 114 students, where he studied Latin, Greek, Mathematics, English composition, the natural sciences, and philosophy. More important than his studies were some of the friendships that he formed while at college. One close friend, Franklin Pierce, would become President of the United States. After finishing his college studies in 1825, Hawthorne again returned to Salem where he went into seclusion with his reading, writing, and solitary walks.

Hawthorne made his first trip to the White Mountains in 1832 after which he traveled through Vermont and New York. At that time a trip to the White Mountains required a certain sense of adventure. Travel was by stage and nights were spent at the very simple roadside inns and taverns that then existed there. These travels allowed Hawthorne to observe the habits of the other travelers and the innkeepers, all of whom he would later describe in his writings.

In the years after completing college Hawthorne wrote a number of short stories, but he had a difficult time finding publishers willing to publish them. The stories that he was able to sell, for very modest amounts, were printed in a variety of journals and magazines. This income was insufficient for his needs and in March 1839 Hawthorne accepted a political appointment at the

Boston Customs House working as a measurer of coal and salt. This job lasted only for two years. In April 1841 Hawthorne invested $1,000 in the Brook Farm Institute of Agriculture and Education in West Roxbury, Massachusetts, which can be most simply be described as an early experiment in communal living. For Hawthorne the experiment ended in August 1841, just four months after he had joined the group. The next year, 1842, Hawthorne married Sophia Peabody of Salem, Massachusetts, whom he had met in 1838. Hawthorne and his wife lived in Concord, Massachusetts, until 1845 when they returned to Salem. Between 1845 and 1849 Hawthorne had another political appointment at the Salem Custom House. During these years he published a few short stories, but he was working on what would become his first successful book, *The Scarlet Letter,* which was published in March 1850. Soon after that Hawthorne moved to Lenox, Massachusetts, where he finished writing *The House of Seven Gables,* which was published in 1851. While living in Lenox, Hawthorne met Herman Melville who was writing *Moby Dick,* also published in 1851, and which Melville dedicated to Hawthorne—"In token of my admiration for his genius this work is inscribed to Nathaniel Hawthorne." Though his own writings were more and more successful, Hawthorne was not far from partisan politics. In 1852, Franklin Pierce received the Democratic nomination for President, and Hawthorne responded by writing a campaign biography for his old friend. Following Pierce's election Hawthorne was appointed American Consul in Liverpool, one of the most lucrative patronage jobs of that period. While working in Liverpool, Hawthorne's journals filled many note-

Nathaniel Hawthorne, probably around 1862. The "Brady" photograph, probably taken by Alexander Gardner of the Mathew Brady Studio.

books which would be a resource in his later writings. After leaving Liverpool he spent a short time in Italy before returning to Concord, Massachusetts, in 1860. By 1862 Hawthorne's health had begun to fail, and he became more withdrawn, depressed, and reclusive.

In the spring of 1864 Sophia Hawthorne wanted her husband to go to New Hampshire for a rest. By prior arrangement Hawthorne met Franklin Pierce in Boston on May 11th, and together they traveled by train to Andover, Massachusetts, and then to Pierce's home in Concord, New Hampshire. Pierce and Hawthorne then traveled north towards the White Mountains. After a few days they arrived for the night at the Pemigewasset House in Plymouth, New Hampshire. Very ill, Hawthorne ate little and went to bed in a room adjoining Pierce's. In the early hours of May 19, 1864, Franklin Pierce, a former President of the United States, discovered that Nathaniel Hawthorne, his close friend and an American literary genius, had died in his sleep. A few days later Hawthorne was buried in the Sleepy Hollow Cemetery in Concord, Massachusetts. After his death Sophia Hawthorne continued to publish excerpts from Hawthorne's European notebooks in *Atlantic Monthly*. Franklin Pierce, whose wife and two sons had died earlier, assumed responsibility for the education of Julian Hawthorne.

THE WHITE MOUNTAIN WRITINGS

Hawthorne's studies and travels often provided him with the characters that he included in his writings. The short piece *Sketches from Memory* includes specific references to the Crawford family in addition to descriptions about the other travelers, "a picturesque group"—perhaps Hawthorne's means of expressing some skepticism and scorn for these travelers. This piece is more a narrative of Hawthorne's travels than a story filled with symbolism. It recounts a trip on which he collected information that he would use in *The Ambitious Guest* and *The Great Carbuncle*, a tale that he specifically refers to at the end of this story. In *Sketches from Memory* it is clear how indebted Hawthorne was to others, such as Ethan Alan Crawford, for some of what he writes about.

The Pemigewasset House, Plymouth, New Hampshire.

When Nathaniel Hawthorne first went the White Mountains in 1832 he visited the site of the Willey family disaster south of Crawford Notch. Here, on the night of August 28, 1826, thunderstorms had triggered landslides that devastated the sides of the mountains and killed Samuel Willey, Jr., his wife, their five children, and the two farm workers. When *The Ambitious Guest*, a fictionalized account of the events of that evening, was first published any reader would have quickly recognized the family and the disaster about which it was written. As in Hawthorne's other writings, there is much symbolism in this story—the modesty and independence of the farmer and his family living in the peace and quiet of the isolated mountains, the family gathered around the fire with its warmth and security, the happiness of the daughter and the grandmother's distinctly different happiness, and the solitary, modest, yet ambitious nature of the guest. Ultimately, the Willey family, always together in life and tragically together in death, achieves in its death the immortality that the unknown guest, always alone, had so desired.

Travelers in the nineteenth century were often entertained by the innkeepers with the local folklore. Undoubtedly, when Ethan Alan Crawford told his guests about the White Mountains he would talk about some of the Indian legends. *The Great Carbuncle* is based upon such a legend—a great gem on Mount Washington that is the object of a search by a group of travelers who are staying at the local inn.

Hawthorne's fourth White Mountain story, *The Great Stone Face* was started in 1840 but was not completed for eight years. John Greenleaf Whittier, the editor of *The National Era*, paid Hawthorne $25 when the story was published in 1850. This story is about a system of philosophy given through a series of characterizations of the Profile in Franconia Notch. A man of wealth, a military man, a statesman, (reportedly Hawthorne meant this to be Daniel Webster), and a poet are all acclaimed as fulfilling a philosophy of faith, fellowship, and good works, but all fall short of fulfilling a local prophecy. In August 1881 this story and its author were described as follows in *Harper's Monthly Magazine*:

> The novelist Hawthorne makes this Sphinx of the White Mountains the interpreter of a noble life. For him the Titanic countenance is radiant with majestic benignity. He endows it with a soul, surrounds the colossal brow with the halo of spiritual grandeur, and marshalling his train of phantoms, proceeds to pass inexorable judgment upon them one by one.

Hawthorne's writings are full of both symbolism and American history which he researched extensively, for he must have recognized that associating his stories with real events, places, and people would result in greater appeal and therefore greater profit. His stories are skillfully organized, the settings are meaningful and important, and the symbolism contained in them is evidence of his ability to present the facts of history, a few basic truths, in a controlling and imaginative way.

Tales of the White Mountains

The Notch of the White Mountains from Mt. Crawford Plate #14, from a painting by Godfrey Frankenstein, from William Oakes' *Scenery of the White Mountains*, Boston, 1848. Mt. Willey is the principal mountain in this painting.

Sketches from Memory

THE NOTCH OF THE WHITE MOUNTAINS

IT WAS NOW the middle of September. We had come since sunrise from Bartlett, passing up through the valley of the Saco, which extends between mountainous walls, sometimes with a steep ascent, but often as level as a church aisle. All that day and two preceding ones we had been loitering towards the heart of the White Mountains,—those old crystal hills, whose mysterious brilliancy had gleamed upon our distant wanderings before we thought of visiting them. Height after height had risen and towered one above another till the clouds began to hang below the peaks. Down their slopes were the red pathways of the slides, those avalanches of earth, stones and trees, which descend into the hollows, leaving vestiges of their track hardly to be effaced by the vegetation of ages. We had mountains behind us and mountains on each side, and a group of mightier ones ahead. Still our road went up along the Saco, right towards the centre of that group, as if to climb above the clouds in its passage to the farther region.

In old times the settlers used to be astounded by the inroads of the northern Indians coming down upon them from this mountain rampart through some defile known only to themselves. It is, indeed, a wondrous path. A demon, it might be fancied, or one of the Titans, was travelling up the valley, elbowing the heights carelessly aside as he passed, till at length a great mountain took its stand directly across his intended road. He tarries not for such an obstacle, but, rending it asunder a thousand feet from peak to base, discloses its treasures of hidden minerals, its sunless waters, all the secrets of the mountain's inmost heart, with a mighty fracture of rugged precipices on each side. This is the Notch of the White Hills. Shame on me that I have attempted to describe it by so mean an image—feeling, as I do, that it is one of those symbolic scenes which lead the mind to the sentiment, though not to the conception, of Omnipotence.

We had now reached a narrow passage, which showed almost the appearance of having been cut by human strength and artifice in the solid rock. There was a wall of granite on each side, high and precipitous, especially on our right, and so smooth that a few evergreens could hardly find foothold enough to grow there. This is the entrance, or, in the direction we were going, the extremity, of the romantic defile of the Notch. Before emerging from it, the rattling of wheels

Gate of the Crawford Notch, Picturesque America, 1872, wood engraving.

approached behind us, and a stage-coach rumbled out of the mountain, with seats on top and trunks behind, and a smart driver, in a drab great-coat, touching the wheel horses with the whip-stock and reining in the leaders. To my mind there was a sort of poetry in such an incident, hardly inferior to what would have accompanied the painted array of an Indian war party gliding forth from the same wild chasm. All the passengers, except a very fat lady on the back seat, had alighted. One was a mineralogist, a scientific, green-spectacled figure in black, bearing a heavy hammer, with which he did great damage to the precipices, and put the fragments in his pocket. Another was a well-dressed young man, who carried an opera glass set in gold, and seemed to be making a quotation from some of Byron's rhapsodies on mountain scenery. There was also a trader returning from Portland to the upper part of Vermont; and a fair young girl, with a very faint bloom like one of those pale and delicate flower which sometimes occur among alpine cliffs.

They disappeared, and we followed them, passing through a deep pine forest, which for some miles allowed us to see nothing but its own dismal shade. Towards nightfall, we reached a level amphitheatre, surrounded by a great rampart of hills, which shut out the sunshine long before it left the external world. It was here that we obtained our first view, except at a distance, of the principal group of mountains. They are majestic, and even awful, when contemplated in a proper mood, yet, by their breadth of base and the long ridges which support them, give the idea of immense bulk rather than of towering height. Mount Washington, indeed, looked near to heaven: he was white with

Mount Washington from the Conway Road, Picturesque America, 1872, wood engraving.

snow a mile downward, and had caught the only cloud that was sailing through the atmosphere to veil his head. Let us forget the other names of American statesmen that have been stamped upon these hills, but still call the loftiest—WASHINGTON. Mountains are Earth's undecaying monuments. They must stand while she endures, and never should be consecrated to the mere great men of their own age and country, but to the mighty ones alone, whose glory is universal, and whom all time will render illustrious.

The air, not often sultry in this elevated region, nearly two thousand feet above the sea, was now sharp and cold, like that of a clear November evening in the lowlands. By morning, probably, there would be a frost, if not a snowfall, on the grass and rye, and an icy surface over the standing water. I was glad to perceive a prospect of comfortable quarters in a house which we were approaching, and of pleasant company in the guests who were assembled at the door.

OUR EVENING PARTY
AMONG THE MOUNTAINS

E STOOD IN front of a good substantial farm-house, of old date in that wild country. A sign over the door denoted it to be the White Mountain Post Office,—an establishment which distributes letters and newspapers to perhaps a score of persons, comprising the population of two or three townships among the hills. The broad and weighty antlers of a deer, "a stag of ten," were fastened at the corner of the house; a fox's bushy tail was nailed beneath them; and a huge black paw lay on the ground, newly severed and still bleeding—the trophy of a bear hunt. Among several persons collected about the doorsteps, the most remarkable was a sturdy mountaineer, of six feet two and corresponding bulk, with a heavy set of features, such as might be moulded on his own blacksmith's anvil, but yet indicative of

The Rosebrook Place. Woodblock drawn by Marshall M. Tidd.

mother wit and rough humor. As we appeared, he up-
lifted a tin trumpet, four or five feet long, and blew a
tremendous blast, either in honor of our arrival or to
awaken an echo from the opposite hill.

Ethan Crawford's guests were of such a motley
description as to form quite a picturesque group, seldom seen together except at some place like this, at once
the pleasure house of fashionable tourists and the
homely inn of country travellers. Among the company
at the door were the mineralogist and the owner of the
gold opera glass whom we had encountered in the
Notch; two Georgian gentlemen, who had chilled their
southern blood that morning on the top of Mount
Washington; a physician and his wife from Conway; a
trader of Burlington, and an old squire of the Green
Mountains; and two young married couples, all the way
from Massachusetts, on the matrimonial jaunt. Besides
these strangers, the rugged county of Coos, in which
we were, was represented by half a dozen wood-cut-
ters, who had slain a bear in the forest and smitten off
his paw.

I had joined the party, and had a moment's leisure
to examine them before the echo of Ethan's blast returned from the hill. Not one, but many echoes had
caught up the harsh and tuneless sound, untwisted its
complicated threads, and found a thousand aerial har-
monies in one stern trumpet-tone. It was a distinct yet
distant and dreamlike symphony of melodious instru-
ments, as if an airy band had been hidden on the
hill-side and made faint music at the summons. No
subsequent trial produced so clear, delicate, and spiri-
tual a concert as the first. A field piece was then
discharged from the top of a neighboring hill, and gave

Mount Crawford, near the White Mountains, with the Mt. Crawford House. Plate #2, by Isaac Sprague, for William Oakes' Scenery of the White Mountains, Boston, 1848.

birth to one long reverberation, which ran round the circle of mountains in an unbroken chain of sound and rolled away without a separate echo. After these experiments, the cold atmosphere drove us all into the house, with the keenest appetites for supper.

It did one's heart good to see the great fires that were kindled in the parlor and bar-room, especially the latter, where the fireplace was built of rough stone, and might have contained the trunk of an old tree for backlog. A man keeps a comfortable hearth when his own forest is at his very door. In the parlor, when the evening was fairly set in, we held our hands before our eyes to shield them from the ruddy glow, and began a pleasant variety of conversation. The mineralogist and the physician talked about the invigorating qualities of the mountain air, and its excellent effect on Ethan Crawford's father, an old man of seventy-five, with the unbroken frame of middle life. The two brides and the doctor's wife held a whispered discussion, which, by their frequent titterings and a blush or two, seemed to have reference to the trials or enjoyments of the matrimonial state. The bridegrooms sat together in a corner, rigidly silent, like Quakers whom the spirit moveth not, being still in the odd predicament of bashfulness, towards their own young wives. The Green Mountain squire chose me for his companion, and described the difficulties he had met with half a century ago in travelling from the Connecticut River through the Notch to Conway, now a single day's journey, though it had cost him eighteen. The Georgians held the album between them, and favored us with the few specimens of its contents which they considered ridiculous enough to be worth hearing. One extract met with deserved applause. It was a

"Sonnet to the Snow on Mount Washington," and had been contributed that very afternoon, bearing a signature of great distinction in magazines and annals. The lines were elegant and full of fancy, but too remote from familiar sentiment, and cold as their subject, resembling those curious specimens of crystallized vapor which I observed next day on the mountain-top. The poet was understood to be the young gentleman of the gold opera glass, who heard our laudatory remarks with the composure of a veteran.

Such was our party, and such their ways of amusement. But on a winter evening another set of guests assembled at the hearth where these summer travellers were now sitting. I once had it in contemplation to spend a month hereabouts, in sleighing time, for the sake of studying the yeomen of New England, who then elbow each other through the notch by hundreds, on their way to Portland. There could be no better school for such a place than Ethan Crawford's inn. Let the student go thither in December, sit down with the teamsters at their meals, share their evening merriment, and repose with them at night when every bed has its three occupants, and parlor, bar-room, and kitchen are strewn with slumberers around the fire. Then let him rise before daylight, button his great-coat, muffle up his ears, and stride with the departing caravan a mile or two, to see how sturdily they make head against the blast. A treasure of characteristic traits will repay all inconveniences, even should a frozen nose be of the number.

The conversation of our party soon became more animated and sincere, and we recounted some traditions of the Indians, who believed that the father and

Notch in the mountains, White Mountains by William H. Bartlett for *American Scenery*, London, 1838.

mother of their race were saved from a deluge by ascending the peak of Mount Washington. The children of that pair have been overwhelmed, and found no such refuge. In the mythology of the savage, these mountains were afterwards considered sacred and inaccessible, full of unearthly wonders, illuminated at lofty heights by the blaze of precious stones, and inhabited by deities, who sometimes shrouded themselves in the snow-storm and came down on the lower world. There are few legends more poetical than that of the "Great Carbuncle" of the White Mountains. The belief was communicated to the English settlers, and is hardly yet extinct, that a gem, of such immense size as to be seen shining miles away, hangs from a rock over a clear, deep lake, high up among the hills. They who had once beheld its splendor were enthralled with an unutterable yearning to possess it. But a spirit guarded that inestimable jewel, and bewildered the adventurer with a dark mist from the enchanted lake. Thus life was worn away in the vain search for an unearthly treasure, till at length the deluded one went up the mountain, still sanguine as in youth, but returned no more. On this theme methinks I could frame a tale with a deep moral.

The hearts of the pale-faces would not thrill to these superstitions of the red men, though we spoke of them in the centre of the haunted region. The habits and sentiments of that departed people were too distinct from those of their successors to find much real sympathy. It has often been a matter of regret to me that I was shut out from the most peculiar field of American fiction by an inability to see any romance, or poetry, or grandeur, or beauty in the Indian character, at least till such traits were pointed out by others. I do abhor an Indian story. Yet no writer can be more secure of a permanent place in our literature than the biographer of the Indian chiefs. His subject, as referring to tribes which have mostly vanished from the earth, gives him a right to be placed on a classic shelf, apart from the merits which will sustain him there.

I made inquiries whether, in his researches about these parts, our mineralogist had found the three "Silver Hills" which an Indian sachem sold to an Englishman nearly two hundred years ago, and the treasure of which the posterity of the purchaser have been looking for ever since. But the man of science had ransacked every hill along the Saco, and knew nothing of these prodigious piles of wealth. By this time, as usual with men on the eve of great adventure, we had prolonged our session deep into the night, considering how early we were to set out on our six miles' ride to the foot of Mount Washington. There was now a general breaking up. I scrutinized the faces of the two bridegrooms, and saw but little probability of their leaving the bosom of earthly bliss, in the first week of the honeymoon and at the frosty hour of three, to climb above the clouds; nor when I felt how sharp the wind was as it rushed through a broken pane, and eddied between the chinks of my unplastered chamber, did I anticipate much alacrity on my own part, though we were to seek for the "Great Carbuncle."

The Ambitious Guest

NE SEPTEMBER NIGHT a family had gathered round their hearth, and piled it high with the driftwood of mountain streams, the dry cones of the pine, and the splintered ruins of great trees that had come crashing down the precipice. Up the chimney roared the fire, and brightened the room with its broad blaze. The faces of the father and mother had a sober gladness; the children laughed; the eldest daughter was the image of Happiness at seventeen; and the aged grandmother, who sat knitting in the warmest place, was the image of Happiness grown old. They had found the "herb, heart's-ease," in the bleakest spot of all New England. This family were situated in the Notch of the White Hills, where the wind was sharp throughout the year, and pitilessly cold in the winter,—giving their cottage all its fresh inclemency before it descended on the valley of the Saco. They dwelt in a cold spot and a dangerous one; for a mountain towered above their heads, so steep, that the stones would often rumble down its sides and startle them at midnight.

The daughter had just uttered some simple jest, that filled them all with mirth, when the wind came through the Notch, and seemed to pause before their cottage—rattling the door, with a sound of wailing and lamentation, before it passed into the valley. For a moment it saddened them, though there was nothing unusual in the tones. But the family were glad again when they perceived that the latch was lifted by some traveller, whose footsteps had been unheard amid the dreary blast which heralded his approach, and wailed as he was entering, and went moaning away from the door.

Though they dwelt in such a solitude, these people held daily converse with the world. The romantic pass of the Notch is a great artery, through which the life-blood of internal commerce is continually throbbing between Maine, on one side, and the Green Mountains and the shores of the St. Lawrence, on the other. The stage-coach always drew up before the door of the cottage. The wayfarer, with no companion but his staff, paused here to exchange a word, that the sense of loneliness might not utterly overcome him ere he could pass through the cleft of the mountain, or reach the first house in the valley. And here the teamster on his way to Portland market, would put up for the night; and, if a bachelor, might sit an hour beyond the usual bedtime, and steal a kiss from the mountain maid at parting. It was one of those primitive taverns where the traveller pays only for food and lodging, but meets with a homely kindness beyond all price. When the footsteps were heard, therefore, between the outer door and the inner one, the whole family rose up, grandmother, children, and all, as if about to welcome someone who belonged to them, and whose fate was linked with theirs.

The door was opened by a young man. His face at first wore the melancholy expression, almost despondency, of one who travels a wild and bleak road, at nightfall and alone, but soon brightened up when he saw the kindly warmth of his reception. He felt his heart spring forward to meet them all, from the old woman, who wiped a chair with her apron, to the little child that held out its arms to him. One glance and smile placed the stranger on a footing of innocent familiarity with the eldest daughter.

"Ah, this fire is the right thing!" cried he; "especially when there is such a pleasant circle round it. I am quite benumbed; for the Notch is just like the pipe of a great pair of bellows; it has blown a terrible blast in my face all the way from Bartlett."

"Then you are going towards Vermont?" said the master of the house, as he helped to take a light knapsack off the young man's shoulders.

"Yes; to Burlington, and far enough beyond," replied he. "I meant to have been at Ethan Crawford's tonight; but a pedestrian lingers along such a road as this. It is no matter; for, when I saw this good fire, and all your cheerfull faces, I felt as if you had kindled it on purpose for me, and were waiting my arrival. So I shall sit down among you, and make myself at home."

The frank-hearted stranger had just drawn his chair to the fire when something like a heavy footstep was heard without, rushing down the steep side of the mountain, as with long and rapid strides, and taking such a leap in passing the cottage as to strike the opposite precipice. The family held their breath, because they knew the sound, and their guest held his by instinct.

"The old mountain has thrown a stone at us, for

fear we should forget him," said the landlord, recovering himself. "He sometimes nods his head and threatens to come down; but we are old neighbors, and agree together pretty well upon the whole. Besides we have a sure place of refuge hard by if he should be coming in good earnest."

Let us now suppose the stranger to have finished his supper of bear's meat; and, by his natural felicity of manner, to have placed himself on a footing of kindness with the whole family, so that they talked as freely together as if he belonged to their mountain brood. He was of a proud, yet gentle spirit—haughty and reserved among the rich and great; but ever ready to stoop his head to the lowly cottage door, and be like a brother or a son at the poor man's fireside. In the household of the Notch he found warmth and simplicity of feeling, the pervading intelligence of New England, and a poetry of native growth, which they had gathered when they little thought of it from the mountain peaks and chasms, and at the very threshold of their romantic and dangerous abode. He had travelled far and alone; his whole life, indeed, had been a solitary path; for, with the lofty caution of his nature, he had kept himself apart from those who might otherwise have been his companions. The family, too, though so kind and hospitable, had that consciousness of unity among themselves, and separation from the world at large, which, in every domestic circle, should still keep a holy place where no stranger may intrude. But this evening a prophetic sympathy impelled the refined and educated youth to pour out his heart before the simple mountaineers, and constrained them to answer him with the same free confidence. And thus it should have been. Is not the kindred of a common fate a closer tie than that of birth?

The secret of the young man's character was a high and abstracted ambition. He could have borne to live an undistinguished life, but not to be forgotten in the grave. Yearning desire had been transformed to hope; and hope, long cherished, had become like certainty, that, obscurely as he journeyed now, a glory was to beam on all his pathway,—though not, perhaps, while he was treading it. But when posterity should gaze back into the gloom of what was now the present, they would trace the brightness of his footsteps, brightening as meaner glories faded, and confess that a gifted one had passed from his cradle to his tomb with none to recognize him.

"As yet," cried the stranger—his cheek glowing and his eye flashing with enthusiasm—"as yet, I have done nothing. Were I to vanish from the earth to-morrow, none would know so much of me as you: that a nameless youth came up at nightfall from the valley of the Saco, and opened his heart to you in the evening, and passed through the Notch by sunrise, and was seen no more. Not a soul would ask, 'Who was he? Whither did the wanderer go?' But I cannot die till I have achieved my destiny. Then, let Death come! I shall have built my monument!"

There was a continual flow of natural emotion, gushing forth amid abstracted reverie, which enabled the family to understand this young man's sentiments, though so foreign from their own. With quick sensibility of the ludicrous, he blushed at the ardor into which he had been betrayed.

"You laugh at me," said he, taking the eldest

daughter's hand, and laughing himself. "You think my ambition as nonsensical as if I were to freeze myself to death on the top of Mount Washington, only that people might spy at me from the country round about. And, truly, that would be a noble pedestal for a man's statue!"

"It is better to sit here by this fire," answered the girl, blushing, "and be comfortable and contented, though nobody thinks about us."

"I suppose," said her father, after a fit of musing, "there is something natural in what the young man says; and if my mind had been turned that way, I might have felt just the same. It is strange, wife, how his talk has set my head running on things that are pretty certain never to come to pass."

"Perhaps they may," observed the wife. "Is the man thinking what he will do when he is a widower?"

"No, no!" cried he, repelling the idea with reproachful kindness. "When I think of your death, Esther, I think of mine too. But I was wishing we had a good farm in Bartlett, or Bethlehem, or Littleton, or some other township round the White Mountains; but not where they could tumble on our heads. I should want to stand well with my neighbors and be called Squire, and sent to General Court for a term or two; for a plain, honest man may do as much good there as a lawyer. And when I should be grown quite an old man, and you an old woman, so as not to be long apart, I might die happy enough in my bed, and leave you all crying around me. A slate gravestone would suit me as well as a marble one—with just my name and age, and a verse of a hymn, and something to let people know that I lived an honest man and died a Christian."

"There now!" exclaimed the stranger; "it is our nature to desire a monument, be it slate or marble, or a pillar of granite, or a glorious memory in the universal heart of man."

"We're in a strange way, to-night," said the wife, with tears in her eyes. "They say it's a sign of something, when folks' minds go a-wandering so. Hark to the children!"

They listened accordingly. The younger children had been put to bed in another room, but with an open door between, so that they could be heard talking busily among themselves. One and all seemed to have caught the infection from the fireside circle, and were outvying each other in wild wishes, and childish projects of what they would do when they came to be men and women. At length a little boy, instead of addressing his brothers and sisters, called out to his mother.

"I'll tell you what I wish, mother," cried he. "I want you and father and grandma'm, and all of us, and the stranger too, to start right away, and go and take a drink out of the basin of the Flume!"

Nobody could help laughing at the child's notion of leaving a warm bed, and dragging them from a cheerful fire, to visit the basin of the Flume,—a brook, which tumbles over the precipice, deep within the Notch. The boy had hardly spoken when a wagon rattled along the road, and stopped a moment before the door. It appeared to contain two or three men, who were cheering their hearts with the rough chorus of a song, which resounded, in broken notes, between the cliffs, while the singers hesitated whether to continue their journey or put up here for the night.

"Father," said the girl, "they are calling you by name."

But the good man doubted whether they had really called him, and was unwilling to show himself too solicitous of gain by inviting people to patronize his house. He therefore did not hurry to the door; and the lash being soon applied, the travellers plunged into the Notch, still singing and laughing, though their music and mirth came back drearily from the heart of the mountain.

"There, mother!" cried the boy, again. "They'd have given us a ride to the Flume."

Again they laughed at the child's pertinacious fancy for a night ramble. But it happened that a light cloud passed over the daughter's spirit; she looked gravely into the fire, and drew a breath that was almost a sigh. It forced its way, in spite of a little struggle to repress it. Then starting and blushing, she looked quickly round the circle, as if they had caught a glimpse into her bosom. The stranger asked what she had been thinking of.

"Nothing," answered she, with a downcast smile. "Only I felt lonesome just then."

"Oh, I have always had a gift of feeling what is in other people's hearts," said he, half seriously. "Shall I tell the secrets of yours? For I know what to think when a young girl shivers by a warm hearth, and complains of lonesomeness at her mother's side. Shall I put these feelings into words?"

"They would not be a girl's feelings any longer if they could be put into words," replied the mountain nymph, laughing, but avoiding his eye.

All this was said apart. Perhaps a germ of love was springing in their hearts, so pure that it might blossom in Paradise, since it could not be matured on earth; for women worship such gentle dignity as his; and the proud, contemplative, yet kindly soul is oftenest captivated by simplicity like hers. But while they spoke softly, and he was watching the happy sadness, the lightsome shadows, the shy yearnings of a maiden's nature, the wind through the Notch took a deeper and drearier sound. It seemed, as the fanciful stranger said, like the choral strain of the spirits of the blast, who in old Indian times had their dwelling among these mountains, and made their heights and recesses a sacred region. There was a wail along the road, as if a funeral were passing. To chase away the gloom, the family threw pine branches on their fire, till the dry leaves crackled and the flame arose, discovering once again a scene of peace and humble happiness. The light hovered about them fondly, and caressed them all. There were the little faces of the children, peeping from their bed apart, and here the father's frame of strength, the mother's subdued and careful mien, the high-browed youth, the budding girl, and the good old grandam, still knitting in the warmest place. The aged woman looked up from her task, and, with fingers ever busy, was the next to speak.

"Old folks have their notions," said she, "as well as young ones. You've been wishing and planning; and letting your heads run on one thing and another, till you've set my mind a-wandering too. Now what should an old woman wish for, when she can go but a step or two before she comes to her grave? Children, it will haunt me night and day till I tell you."

"What is it, mother?" cried the husband and wife at once.

Then the old woman, with an air of mystery which

drew the circle closer round the fire, informed them that she had provided her grave-clothes some years before,—a nice linen shroud, a cap with a muslin ruff, and everything of a finer sort than she had worn since her wedding day. But this evening an old superstition had strangely recurred to her. It used to be said, in her younger days, that if anything were amiss with a corpse, if only the ruff were not smooth, or the cap did not set right, the corpse in the coffin and beneath the clods would strive to put up its cold hands and arrange it. The bare thought made her nervous.

"Don't talk so, grandmother!" said the girl, shuddering.

"Now,"—continued the old woman, with singular earnestness, yet smiling strangely at her own folly,— "I want one of you, my children—when your mother is dressed and in the coffin—I want one of you to hold a looking-glass over my face. Who knows but I may take a glimpse at myself, and see whether all's right?"

"Old and young, we dream of graves and monuments," murmured the stranger youth. "I wonder how mariners feel when the ship is sinking, and they, unknown and undistinguished, are to be buried together in the ocean—that wide and nameless sepulchre?"

For a moment, the old woman's ghastly conception so engrossed the minds of her hearers that a sound abroad in the night, rising like the roar of a blast, had grown broad, deep, and terrible, before the fated group were conscious of it. The house and all within it trembled; the foundations of the earth seemed to be shaken, as if this awful sound were the peal of the last trump. Young and old exchanged one wild glance, and remained an instant, pale, affrighted, without utterance, or power to move. Then the same shriek burst simultaneously from all their lips.

"The Slide! The Slide!"

The simplest words must intimate, but not portray, the unutterable horror of the catastrophe. The victims rushed from their cottage, and sought refuge in what they deemed a safer spot—where, in contemplation of such an emergency, a sort of barrier had been reared. Alas! they had quitted their security, and fled right into the pathway of destruction. Down came the whole side of the mountain, in a cataract of ruin. Just before it reached the house, the stream broke into two branches—shivered not a window there but overwhelmed the whole vicinity, blocked up the road, and annihilated everything in its dreadful course. Long ere the thunder of the great Slide had ceased to roar among the mountains, the mortal agony had been endured, and the victims were at peace. Their bodies were never found.

The next morning, the light smoke was seen stealing from the cottage chimney up the mountain side. Within, the fire was yet smouldering on the hearth, and the chairs in a circle round it, as if the inhabitants had but gone forth to view the devastation of the Slide, and would shortly return, to thank Heaven for their miraculous escape. All had left separate tokens, by which those who had known the family were made to shed a tear for each. Who has not heard their name? The story has been told far and wide, and will forever be a legend of these mountains. Poets have sung their fate.

There were circumstances which led some to suppose that a stranger had been received into the cottage on this awful night, and had shared the catastrophe of all its inmates. Others denied that there were sufficient grounds for such a conjecture. Woe for the high-souled youth, with his dream of Earthly Immortality! His name and person utterly unknown; his history, his way of life, his plans, a mystery never to be solved, his death and his existence equally a doubt! Whose was the agony of that death moment?

The Great Carbuncle

A MYSTERY OF
THE WHITE MOUNTAINS

AT NIGHTFALL, ONCE, in the olden time, on the rugged side of one of the Crystal Hills, a party of adventurers were refreshing themselves, after a toilsome and fruitless quest for the Great Carbuncle. They had come thither, not as friends nor partners in the enterprise, but each, save one youthful pair, impelled by his own selfish and solitary longing for this wondrous gem. Their feeling of brotherhood, however, was strong enough to induce them to contribute a mutual aid in building a rude hut of branches, and kindling a great fire of shattered pines, that had drifted down the headlong current of the Amonoosuck, on the lower bank of which they were

The Indian tradition, on which this somewhat extravagant tale is founded, is both too wild and too beautiful to be adequately wrought up in prose. Sullivan, in his *History of Maine*, written since the Revolution, remarks, that even then the existence of the Great Carbuncle was not entirely discredited.

to pass the night. There was but one of their number, perhaps, who had become so estranged from natural sympathies, by the absorbing spell of the pursuit, as to acknowledge no satisfaction at the sight of human faces, in the remote and solitary region whither they had ascended. A vast extent of wilderness lay between them and the nearest settlement, while scant a mile above their heads was that black verge where the hills throw off their shaggy mantle of forest trees, and either robe themselves in clouds, or tower naked into the sky. The roar of the Amonoosuck would have been too awful for endurance, if only a solitary man had listened, while the mountain stream talked with the wind.

The adventurers, therefore, exchanged hospitable greetings, and welcomed one another to the hut, where each man was the host, and all were the guests of the whole company. They spread their individual supplies of food on the flat surface of a rock, and partook of a general repast; at the close of which, a sentiment of good fellowship was perceptible among the party, though repressed by the idea, that the renewed search for the Great Carbuncle must make them strangers again in the morning. Seven men and one young woman, they warmed themselves together at the fire, which extended its bright wall along the whole front of their wigwam. As they observed the various and contrasted figures that made up the assemblage, each man looking like a caricature of himself, in the unsteady light that flickered over him, they came mutually to the conclusion, that an odder society had never met, in city or wilderness, on mountain or plain.

The eldest of the group, a tall, lean, weather-beaten man, some sixty years of age, was clad in the skins of

The White Mountains, from the Giant's Grave, near the Mount Washington House. Plate #1, by Isaac Sprague, from William Oakes' Scenery of the White Mountains, Boston, 1848.

wild animals, whose fashion of dress he did well to imitate, since the deer, the wolf, and the bear, had long been his most intimate companions. He was one of those ill fated mortals, such as the Indians told of, whom, in their early youth, the Great Carbuncle smote with a peculiar madness, and became the passionate dream of their existence. All who visited that region knew him as the Seeker, and by no other name. As none could remember when he first took up the search, there went a fable in the valley of the Saco, that for his inordinate lust after the Great Carbuncle, he had been condemned to wander among the mountains till the end of time, still with the same feverish hopes at sunrise—the same despair at eve. Near this miserable Seeker sat a little elderly personage, wearing a high-crowned hat, shaped somewhat like a crucible. He was from beyond the sea, a Doctor Cacaphodel, who had wilted and dried himself into a mummy by continually stooping over charcoal furnaces, and inhaling unwholesome fumes during his researches in chemistry and alchemy. It was told of him, whether truly or not, that, at the commencement of his studies, he had drained his body of all its richest blood, and wasted it, with other inestimable ingredients, in an unsuccessful experiment—and had never been a well man since. Another of the adventurers was Master Ichabod Pigsnort, a weighty merchant and selectman of Boston, and an elder of the famous Mr. Norton's church. His enemies had a ridiculous story that Master Pigsnort was accustomed to spend a whole hour, after prayer time, every morning and evening, in wallowing naked among an immense quantity of pine-tree shillings, which were the earliest silver coinage of Massachusetts.

The fourth, whom we shall notice, had no name that his companions knew of, and was chiefly distinguished by a sneer that always contorted his thin visage, and by a prodigious pair of spectacles, which were supposed to deform and discolor the whole face of nature, to this gentleman's perception. The fifth adventurer likewise lacked a name, which was the greater pity, as he appeared to be a poet. He was a bright-eyed man, but wofully pined away, which was no more than natural, if, as some people affirmed, his ordinary diet was fog, morning mist, and a slice of the densest cloud within reach, sauced with moonshine, whenever he could get it. Certain it is, that the poetry which flowed from him had a smack of all these dainties. The sixth of the party was a young man of haughty mien, and sat somewhat apart from the rest, wearing his plumed hat loftily among his elders, while the fire glittered on the rich embroidery of his dress and gleamed intensely on the jewelled pommel of his sword. This was the Lord de Vere, who, when at home, was said to spend much of his time in the burial vault of his dead progenitors, rummaging their mouldy coffins in search of all the earthly pride and vain-glory that was hidden among bones and dust; so that, besides his own share, he had the collected haughtiness of his whole line of ancestry.

Lastly there was a handsome youth in rustic garb, and by his side a blooming little person, in whom a delicate shade of maiden reserve was just melting into the rich glow of a young wife's affection. Her name was Hannah, and her husband's Matthew; two homely names, yet well enough adapted to the simple pair, who seemed strangely out of place among the whimsical fraternity whose wits had been set agog by the Great Carbuncle.

Beneath the shelter of one hut, in the bright blaze of the same fire, sat this varied group of adventurers, all so intent upon a single object, that, of whatever else they began to speak, their closing words were sure to be illuminated with the Great Carbuncle. Several related the circumstances that brought them thither. One had listened to a traveller's tale of this marvellous stone in his own distant country, and had immediately been seized with such a thirst for beholding it as could only be quenched in its intensest lustre. Another, so long ago as when the famous Captain Smith visited these coasts, had seen it blazing far at sea, and had felt no rest in all the intervening years till now that he took up the search. A third, being encamped on a hunting expedition full forty miles south of the White Mountains, awoke at midnight, and beheld the Great Carbuncle gleaming like a meteor, so that the shadows of the trees fell backward from it. They spoke of the innumerable attempts which had been made to reach the spot, and of the singular fatality which had hitherto withheld success from all adventurers, though it might seem so easy to follow to its source a light that overpowered the moon, and almost matched the sun. It was observable that each smiled scornfully at the madness of every other in anticipating better fortune than the past, yet nourished a scarcely hidden conviction that he would himself be the favored one. As if to allay their too sanguine hopes, they recurred to the Indian traditions that a spirit kept watch about the gem, and bewildered those who sought it, either by removing it from peak to peak of the higher hills, or by calling up a mist from the enchanted lake over which it hung. But these tales were deemed unworthy of credit, all professing to believe that the search had been baffled by want of sagacity or perseverance in the adventurers, or such other causes as might naturally obstruct the passage to any given point, among the intricacies of forest, valley, and mountain.

In a pause of the conversation the wearer of the prodigious spectacles looked round upon the party, making each individual, in turn, the object of the sneer which invariably dwelt upon his countenance.

"So, fellow-pilgrims," said he, "here we are, seven wise men, and one fair damsel—who, doubtless, is as wise as any graybeard of the company: here we are, I say, all bound on the same goodly enterprise. Methinks, now, it were not amiss that each of us declare what he proposes to do with the Great Carbuncle, provided he have the good hap to clutch it. What says our friend in the bear skin? How mean you, good sir, to enjoy the prize which you have been seeking, the Lord knows how long, among the Crystal Hills?"

"How enjoy it!" exclaimed the aged Seeker, bitterly. "I hope for no enjoyment from it; that folly has passed long ago! I keep up the search for this accursed stone because the vain ambition of my youth has become a fate upon me in old age. The pursuit alone is my strength,—the energy of my soul,—the warmth of my blood,—and the pith and marrow of my bones! Were I to turn my back upon it I should fall down dead on the hither side of the Notch, which is the gateway of this mountain region. Yet, not to have my wasted lifetime back again, would I give up my hopes of the Great Carbuncle! Having found it, I shall bear it to a certain cavern that I wot of, and there, grasping it in my arms, lie down and die, and keep it buried with me forever."

"O wretch, regardless of the interests of science!" cried Doctor Cacaphodel, with philosophic indignation. "Thou art not worthy to behold, even from afar off, the lustre of this most precious gem that ever was concocted in the laboratory of Nature. Mine is the sole purpose for which a wise man may desire the possession of the Great Carbuncle. Immediately on obtaining it—for I have a presentiment, good people, that the prize is reserved to crown my scientific reputation—I shall return to Europe, and employ my remaining years in reducing it to its first elements. A portion of the stone will I grind to impalpable powder; other parts shall be dissolved in acids, or whatever solvents will act upon so admirable a composition; and the remainder I design to melt in the crucible, or set on fire with the blow-pipe. By these various methods, I shall gain an accurate analysis, and finally bestow the result of my labors upon the world in a folio volume."

"Excellent!" quoth the man with the spectacles. "Nor need you hesitate, learned Sir, on account of the necessary destruction of the gem; since the perusal of your folio may teach every mother's son of us to concoct a Great Carbuncle of his own."

"But, verily," said Master Ichabod Pigsnort, "for mine own part I object to the making of these counterfeits, as being calculated to reduce the marketable value of the true gem. I tell ye frankly, Sirs, I have an interest in keeping up the price. Here have I quitted my regular traffic, leaving my warehouse in the care of my clerks, and putting my credit to great hazard, and, furthermore, have put myself in peril of death or captivity by the accursed heathen savages—and all this without daring to ask the prayers of the congregation, because

the quest for the Great Carbuncle is deemed little better than a traffic with the Evil One. Now think ye that
I would have done this grievous wrong to my soul,
body, reputation, and estate, without a reasonable
chance of profit?"

"Not I, pious Master Pigsnort," said the man with
the spectacles. "I never laid such a great folly to thy
charge."

"Truly, I hope not," said the merchant. "Now, as
touching this Great Carbuncle, I am free to own that I
have never had a glimpse of it; but be it only the hun-
dredth part so bright as people tell, it will surely
outvalue the Great Mogul's best diamond, which he
holds at an incalculable sum. Wherefore, I am minded
to put the Great Carbuncle on shipboard, and voyage
with it to England, France, Spain, Italy, or into
Heathendom, if Providence should send me thither,
and, in a word, dispose of the gem to the best bidder
among the potentates of the earth, that he may place it
among his crown jewels. If any of ye have a wiser plan,
let him expound it."

"That have I, thou sordid man!" exclaimed the poet.
"Dost thou desire nothing brighter than gold that thou
wouldst transmute all this ethereal lustre into such dross
as thou wallowest in already? For myself, hiding the
jewel under my cloak, I shall hie me back to my attic
chamber, in one of the darksome alleys of London.
There, night and day, will I gaze upon it—my soul shall
drink its radiance—it shall be diffused throughout my
intellectual powers, and gleam brightly in every line of
poesy that I indite. Thus, long ages after I am gone, the
splendor of the Great Carbuncle will blaze around my
name!"

"Well said, Master Poet!" cried he of the spectacles. "Hide it under thy cloak, sayest thou? Why, it will gleam through the holes, and make thee look like a jack-o'lantern!"

"To think!" ejaculated the Lord de Vere, rather to himself than his companions, the best of whom he held utterly unworthy of his intercourse—"to think that a fellow in a tattered cloak should talk of conveying the Great Carbuncle to a garret in Grub Street! Have not I resolved within myself that the whole earth contains no fitter ornament for the great hall of my ancestral castle? There shall it flame for ages, making a noonday of midnight, glittering on the suits of armor, the banners, and escutcheons, that hang around the wall, and keeping bright the memory of heroes. Wherefore have all other adventurers sought the prize in vain, but that I might win it, and make it a symbol of the glories of our lofty line? And never, on the diadem of the White Mountains, did the Great Carbuncle hold a place half so honored as is reserved for it in the hall of the De Veres!"

"It is a noble thought," said the Cynic, with an obsequious sneer. "Yet, might I presume to say so, the gem would make a rare sepulchral lamp, and would display the glories of your lordship's progenitors more truly in the ancestral vault than in the castle hall."

"Nay, forsooth," observed Matthew, the young rustic, who sat hand in hand with his bride, "the gentleman has bethought himself of a profitable use for this bright stone. Hannah here and I are seeking it for a like purpose."

"How, fellow!" exclaimed his lordship, in surprise. "What castle hall hast thou to hang it in?"

"No castle," replied Matthew, "but as neat a cottage as any within sight of the Crystal Hills. Ye must know, friends, that Hannah and I, being wedded the last week, have taken up the search of the Great Carbuncle, because we shall need its light in the long winter evenings; and it will be such a pretty thing to show the neighbors when they visit us. It will shine through the house so that we may pick up a pin in any corner, and will set all the windows a-glowing as if there were a great fire of pine knots in the chimney. And then how pleasant, when we awake in the night, to be able to see one another's faces!"

There was a general smile among the adventurers at the simplicity of the young couple's project in regard to this wondrous and invaluable stone, with which the greatest monarch on earth might have been proud to adorn his palace. Especially the man with spectacles, who had sneered at all the company in turn, now twisted his visage into such an expression of ill-natured mirth, that Matthew asked him, rather peevishly, what he himself meant to do with the Great Carbuncle.

"The Great Carbuncle!" answered the Cynic, with ineffable scorn. "Why, you blockhead, there is no such thing in *rerum natura*. I have come three thousand miles, and am resolved to set my foot on every peak of these mountains, and poke my head into every chasm, for the sole purpose of demonstrating to the satisfaction of any man, one whit less an ass than thyself, that the Great Carbuncle is all a humbug!"

Vain and foolish were the motives that had brought most of the adventurers to the Crystal Hills; but none so vain, so foolish, and so impious too, as that of the scoffer with the prodigious spectacles. He was one of those wretched and evil men whose yearnings are downward to the darkness, instead of Heavenward, and who, could they but extinguish the lights which God hath kindled for us, would count the midnight gloom their chiefest glory. As the Cynic spoke, several of the party were startled by a gleam of red splendor, that showed the huge shapes of the surrounding mountains and the rock-bestrewn bed of the turbulent river with an illumination unlike that of their fire, on the trunks and black boughs of the forest trees. They listened for the roll of thunder, but heard nothing, and were glad that the tempest came not near them. The stars, those dial-points of heaven, now warned the adventurers to close their eyes on the blazing logs, and open them, in dreams, to the glow of the Great Carbuncle.

The young married couple had taken their lodgings in the farthest corner of the wigwam, and were separated from the rest of the party by a curtain of curiously woven twigs, such as might have hung, in deep festoons, around the bridal bower of Eve. The modest little wife had wrought this piece of tapestry while the other guests were talking. She and her husband fell asleep with hands tenderly clasped, and awoke, from visions of unearthly radiance, to meet the more blessed light of one another's eyes. They awoke at the same instant, and with one happy smile beaming over their two faces, which grew brighter with their consciousness of the reality of life and love. But no sooner did she recollect where they were, than the bride peeped through the interstices of the leafy curtain, and saw that the outer room of the hut was deserted.

"Up, dear Matthew !" cried she, in haste. "The strange folk are all gone! Up, this very minute, or we

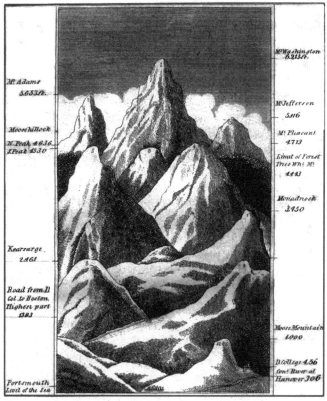

Comparative View of the Heights of Mountains &c. in N. Hampshire. From John Farmer and Jacob Moore's *Gazetteer of the State of New Hampshire,* Concord, N. H., 1823.

shall lose the Great Carbuncle!"

In truth, so little did these poor young people deserve the mighty prize which had lured them thither, that they had slept peacefully all night, and till the summits of the hills were glittering with sunshine; while the other adventurers had tossed their limbs in feverish wakefulness, or dreamed of climbing precipices, and set off to realize their dreams with the earliest peep of dawn. But Matthew and Hannah, after their calm rest, were as light as two young deer, and merely stopped to say their prayers and wash themselves in a cold pool of the Amonoosuck, and then to taste a morsel of food, ere they turned their faces to the mountain-side. It was a sweet emblem of conjugal affection, as they toiled up the difficult ascent, gathering strength from the mutual aid which they afforded. After several little accidents, such as a torn robe, a lost shoe, and the entanglement of Hannah's hair in a bough, they reached the upper verge of the forest, and were now to pursue a more adventurous course. The innumerable trunks and heavy foliage of the trees had hitherto shut in their thoughts, which now shrank affrighted from the region of wind, and cloud, and naked rocks, and desolate sunshine, that rose immeasurably above them. They gazed back at the obscure wilderness which they had traversed, and longed to be buried again in its depths, rather than trust themselves to so vast and visible a solitude.

"Shall we go on?" said Matthew, throwing his arm round Hannah's waist, both to protect her, and to comfort his heart by drawing her close to it.

But the little bride, simple as she was, had a woman's love of jewels, and could not forego the hope of possessing the very brightest in the world, in spite of the perils with which it must be won.

"Let us climb a little higher," whispered she, yet tremulously, as she turned her face upward to the lonely sky.

"Come, then," said Matthew, mustering his manly courage, and drawing her along with him; for she became timid again, the moment that he grew bold.

And upward, accordingly, went the pilgrims of the Great Carbuncle, now treading upon the tops and thickly interwoven branches of dwarf pines, which, by the growth of centuries, though mossy with age, had barely reached three feet in altitude. Next, they came to masses and fragments of naked rock heaped confusedly together, like a cairn reared by giants in memory of a giant chief. In this bleak realm of upper air nothing breathed, nothing grew; there was no life but what was concentrated in their two hearts; they had climbed so high that Nature herself seemed no longer to keep them company. She lingered beneath them, within the verge of the forest trees, and sent a farewell glance after her children, as they strayed where her own green footprints had never been. But soon they were to be hidden from her eye. Densely and dark the mists began to gather below, casting black spots of shadow on the vast landscape, and sailing heavily to one centre, as if the loftiest mountain peak had summoned a council of its kindred clouds. Finally, the vapors welded themselves, as it were, into a mass, presenting the appearance of a pavement over which the wanderers might have trodden, but where they would vainly have sought an avenue to the blessed earth which they had lost. And the lovers yearned to behold that green earth again, more intensely, alas! than, beneath a clouded sky, they had ever desired a glimpse of Heaven. They even felt it a relief to their desolation when the mists, creeping gradually up the mountain, concealed its lonely peak, and thus annihilated, at least for them, the whole region of visible space. But they drew closer together, with a fond and melancholy gaze, dreading lest the universal cloud should snatch them from each other's sight.

Still, perhaps, they would have been resolute to climb as far and as high, between earth and heaven, as they could find foothold, if Hannah's strength had not begun to fail, and with that, her courage also. Her breath grew short. She refused to burthen her husband with her weight, but often tottered against his side, and recovered herself each time by a feebler effort. At last, she sank down on one of the rocky steps of the acclivity.

"We are lost, dear Matthew," said she, mournfully. "We shall never find our way to the earth again. And, oh, how happy we might have been in our cottage!"

"Dear heart!—we will yet be happy there," answered Matthew. "Look! In this direction, the sunshine penetrates the dismal mist. By its aid, I can direct our course to the passage of the Notch. Let us go back, love, and dream no more of the Great Carbuncle!"

"The sun cannot be yonder," said Hannah, with despondence. "By this time it must be noon. If there could ever be any sunshine here, it would come from above our heads."

"But look!" repeated Matthew, in a somewhat altered tone. "It is brightening every moment. If not sunshine, what can it be?"

Nor could the young bride any longer deny that a radiance was breaking through the mist, and changing its dim hue to a dusky red, which continually grew more vivid, as if brilliant particles were interfused with the gloom. Now, also, the cloud began to roll away from the mountain, while, as it heavily withdrew, one object after another started out of its impenetrable obscurity into sight, with precisely the effect of a new creation, before the indistinctness of the old chaos had been completely swallowed up. As the process went on, they saw the gleaming of water close at their feet, and found themselves on the very border of a mountain lake, deep, bright, clear, and calmly beautiful, spreading from brim to brim of a basin that had been scooped out of the solid rock. A ray of glory flashed across its surface. The pilgrims looked whence it should proceed, but closed their eyes with a thrill of awful admiration, to exclude the fervid splendor that glowed from the brow of a cliff impending over the enchanted lake. For the simple pair had reached that lake of mystery, and found the long-sought shrine of the Great Carbuncle!

They threw their arms around each other, and trembled at their own success; for, as the legends of this wondrous gem rushed thick upon their memory, they felt themselves marked out by fate—and the consciousness was fearful. Often, from childhood upward, they had seen it shining like a distant star. And now that star was throwing its intensest lustre on their hearts. They seemed changed to one another's eyes, in the red brilliancy that flamed upon their cheeks, while it lent the same fire to the lake, the rocks, and sky, and to the mists which had rolled back before its power. But, with their next glance, they beheld an object that drew their attention even from the mighty stone. At the base of the cliff, directly beneath the Great Carbuncle, appeared the figure of a man, with his arms extended in the act of climbing, and his face turned upward, as if to drink the full gush of splendor. But he stirred not, no more than if changed to marble.

"It is the Seeker," whispered Hannah, convulsively grasping her husband's arm. "Matthew, he is dead."

"The joy of success has killed him," replied Matthew, trembling violently. "Or, perhaps, the very light of the Great Carbuncle was death."

"The Great Carbuncle," cried a peevish voice behind them. "The Great Humbug! If you have found it, prithee point it out to me."

They turned their heads, and there was the Cynic, with his prodigious spectacles set carefully on his nose, staring now at the lake, now at the rocks, now at the distant masses of vapor, now right at the Great Carbuncle itself, yet seemingly as unconscious of its light as if all the scattered clouds were condensed about his person. Though its radiance actually threw the shadow of the unbeliever at his own feet, as he turned his back upon the glorious jewel, he would not be convinced that there was the least glimmer there.

"Where is your Great Humbug?" he repeated. "I challenge you to make me see it!"

"There," said Matthew, incensed at such perverse blindness, and turning the Cynic round towards the illuminated cliff. "Take off those abominable spectacles, and you cannot help seeing it!"

Now these colored spectacles probably darkened the Cynic's sight, in at least as great a degree as the smoked glasses through which people gaze at an eclipse. With resolute bravado, however, he snatched them from his nose, and fixed a bold stare full upon the ruddy blaze of the Great Carbuncle. But scarcely had he encountered it, when, with a deep, shuddering groan, he dropped his head, and pressed both hands across his miserable eyes. Thenceforth there was, in very truth, no light of the Great Carbuncle, nor any other light on earth, nor light of heaven itself, for the poor Cynic. So long accustomed to view all objects through a medium that deprived them of every glimpse of brightness, a single flash of so glorious a phenomenon, striking upon his naked vision, had blinded him forever.

"Matthew," said Hannah clinging to him, "let us go hence!"

Matthew saw that she was faint, and kneeling down, supported her in his arms, while he threw some of the thrillingly cold water of the enchanted lake upon her face and bosom. It revived her, but could not renovate her courage.

"Yes, dearest!" cried Matthew, pressing her tremulous form to his breast,—"we will go hence, and return to our humble cottage. The blessed sunshine and the quiet moonlight shall come through our window. We will kindle the cheerful glow of our hearth, at eventide, and be happy in its light. But never again will we desire more light than all the world may share with us."

"No," said his bride, "for how could we live day, or sleep by night, in this awful blaze of the Great Carbuncle!"

Out of the hollow of their hands, they drank each a draught from the lake, which presented them its waters uncontaminated by an earthly lip. Then, lending their guidance to the blinded Cynic, who uttered not a word, and even stifled his groans in his own most wretched heart, they began to descend the mountain. Yet, as they left the shore, till then untrodden, of the spirit's lake, they threw a farewell glance towards the cliff, and beheld the vapors gathering in dense volumes, through which the gem burned duskily.

As touching the other pilgrims of the Great Carbuncle, the legend goes on to tell, that the worshipful Master Ichabod Pigsnort soon gave up the quest, as desperate speculation, and wisely resolved to betake himself again to his warehouse, near the town-dock, in Boston. But, as he passed through the Notch of the mountains, a war party of Indians captured our unlucky merchant, and carried him to Montreal, there holding him in bondage, till, by the payment of heavy ransom, he had wofully subtracted from his hoard of pine-tree shillings. By his long absence, moreover, his affairs had become so disordered that, for the rest of his life, instead of wallowing in silver, he had seldom a sixpence worth of copper. Doctor Cacaphodel, the alchemist, returned to his laboratory with a prodigious fragment of granite, which he ground to powder, dissolved in acids, melted in the crucible, and burnt with the blow-pipe, and published the results of his experiments in one of the heaviest folios of the day. And, for all these purposes, the gem itself could not have answered better than the granite. The poet, by a somewhat similar mistake, made prize of a great piece of ice, which he found in a sunless chasm of the mountains, and swore that it corresponded, in all points, with his idea of the Great Carbuncle. The critics say, that, if his poetry lacked the splendor of the gem, it retained all the coldness of the ice. The Lord de Vere went back to his ancestral hall, where he contented himself with a wax-lighted chandelier, and filled, in due course of time, another coffin in the ancestral vault. As the funeral torches gleamed within that dark receptacle, there was no need of the Great Carbuncle to show the vanity of earthly pomp.

The Cynic, having cast aside his spectacles, wandered about the world, a miserable object, and was punished with an agonizing desire of light, for the wilful blindness of his former life. The whole night long, he would lift his splendor-blasted orbs to the moon and stars; he turned his face eastward, at sunrise, as duly as a Persian idolater; he made a pilgrimage to Rome, to witness the magnificent illumination of St. Peter's Church; and finally perished in the great fire of London, into the midst of which be had thrust himself, with the desperate idea of catching one feeble ray from the blaze that was kindling earth and heaven.

Matthew and his bride spent many peaceful years, and were fond of telling the legend of the Great Carbuncle. The tale, however, towards the close of their lengthened lives, did not meet with the full credence that had been accorded to it by those who remembered the ancient lustre of the gem. For it is affirmed that, from the hour when two mortals had shown themselves so simply wise as to reject a jewel which would have dimmed all earthly things, its splendor waned. When other pilgrims reached the cliff, they found only an opaque stone, with particles of mica glittering on its surface. There is also a tradition that, as the youthful pair departed, the gem was loosened from the forehead of the cliff, and fell into the enchanted lake, and that, at noontide, the Seeker's form may still be seen to bend over its quenchless gleam.

Some few believe that this inestimable stone is blazing, as of old, and say that they have caught its radiance, like a flash of summer lightning, far down the valley of the Saco. And be it owned that, many a mile from the Crystal Hills, I saw a wondrous light around their summits, and was lured, by the faith of poesy, to be the latest pilgrim of the GREAT CARBUNCLE.

Profile Mountain at Franconia, New Hampshire. Plate #9, by Isaac Sprague, from William Oakes' *Scenery of the White Mountains,* Boston, 1848.

The Great
Stone Face

NE AFTERNOON, WHEN the sun was going down, a mother and her little boy sat at the door of their cottage, talking about the Great Stone Face. They had but to lift their eyes, and there it was plainly to be seen, though miles away, with the sunshine brightening all its features.

And what was the Great Stone Face?

Embosomed amongst a family of lofty mountains, there was a valley so spacious that it contained many thousand inhabitants. Some of these good people dwelt in log-huts, with the black forest all around them, on the steep and difficult hill-sides. Others had their homes in comfortable farm-houses, and cultivated the rich soil on the gentle slopes or level surfaces of the valley. Others, again, were congregated into populous villages, where some wild, highland rivulet, tumbling down from its birthplace in the upper mountain region, had been caught and tamed by human cunning, and compelled to turn the machinery of cotton factories. The inhabitants of this valley, in short, were numerous, and

49

of many modes of life. But all of them, grown people and children, had a kind of familiarity with the Great Stone Face, although some possessed the gift of distinguishing this grand natural phenomenon more perfectly than many of their neighbors.

The Great Stone Face, then, was a work of Nature in her mood of majestic playfulness, formed on the perpendicular side of a mountain by some immense rocks, which had been thrown together in such a position as, when viewed at a proper distance, precisely to resemble the features of the human countenance. It seemed as if an enormous giant, or a Titan, had sculptured his own likeness on the precipice. There was the broad arch of the forehead, a hundred feet in height; the nose, with its long bridge; and the vast lips, which, if they could have spoken, would have rolled their thunder accents from one end of the valley to the other. True it is, that if the spectator approached too near, he lost the outline of the gigantic visage, and could discern only a heap of ponderous and gigantic rocks, piled in chaotic ruin one upon another. Retracing his steps, however, the wondrous features would again be seen; and the farther he withdrew from them, the more like a human face, with all its original divinity intact, did they appear; until, as it grew dim in the distance, with the clouds and glorified vapor of the mountains clustering about it, the Great Stone Face seemed positively to be alive.

It was a happy lot for children to grow up to manhood or womanhood with the Great Stone Face before their eyes, for all the features were noble, and the expression was at once grand and sweet, as if it were the glow of a vast, warm heart, that embraced all mankind

in its affections, and had room for more. It was an education only to look at it. According to the belief of many
people, the valley owed much of its fertility to this benign aspect that was continually beaming over it,
illuminating the clouds, and infusing its tenderness into
the sunshine.

As we began with saying, a mother and her little
boy sat at their cottage-door, gazing at the Great Stone
Face, and talking about it. The child's name was Ernest.

"Mother," said he, while the Titanic visage smiled
on him, "I wish that it could speak, for it looks so very
kindly that its voice must needs be pleasant. If I were
to see a man with such a face, I should love him dearly."

"If an old prophecy should come to pass," answered
his mother, "we may see a man, some time or other,
with exactly such a face as that."

"What prophecy do you mean, dear mother?" ea-
gerly inquired Ernest. "Pray tell me all about it!"

So his mother told him a story that her own mother
had told to her, when she herself was younger than little
Ernest; a story, not of things that were past, but of what
was yet to come; a story, nevertheless, so very old, that
even the Indians, who formerly inhabited this valley,
had heard it from their forefathers, to whom, as they
affirmed, it had been murmured by the mountain streams,
and whispered by the wind among the tree-tops. The
purport was, that, at some future day, a child should be
born hereabouts, who was destined to become the greatest and noblest personage of his time, and whose
countenance, in manhood, should bear an exact resem-

blance to the Great Stone Face. Not a few old-fashioned people, and young ones likewise, in the ardor of their hopes, still cherished an enduring faith in this old prophecy. But others, who had seen more of the world, had watched and waited till they were weary, and had beheld no man with such a face, nor any man that proved to be much greater or nobler than his neighbors, concluded it to be nothing but an idle tale. At all events, the great man of the prophecy had not yet appeared.

"O mother, dear mother!" cried Ernest, clapping his hands above his head, "I do hope that I shall live to see him!"

His mother was an affectionate and thoughtful woman, and felt that it was wisest not to discourage the generous hopes of her little boy. So she only said to him, "Perhaps you may."

And Ernest never forgot the story that his mother told him. It was always in his mind, whenever he looked upon the Great Stone Face. He spent his childhood in the log-cottage where he was born, and was dutiful to his mother, and helpful to her in many things, assisting her much with his little hands, and more with his loving heart. In this manner, from a happy yet often pensive child, he grew up to be a mild, quiet, unobtrusive boy, and sun-browned with labor in the fields, but with more intelligence brightening his aspect than is seen in many lads who have been taught at famous schools. Yet Ernest had had no teacher, save only that the Great Stone Face became one to him. When the toil of the day was over, he would gaze at it for hours, until he began to imagine that those vast features recognized him, and gave him a smile of kindness and

Old Man of the Mountain—Detroit Photographic Co.

encouragement, responsive to his own look of veneration. We must not take upon us to affirm that this was a mistake, although the Face may have looked no more kindly at Ernest than at all the world besides. But the secret was that the boy's tender and confiding simplicity discerned what other people could not see; and thus the love, which was meant for all, became his peculiar portion.

About this time there went a rumor throughout the valley, that the great man, foretold from ages long ago, who was to bear a resemblance to the Great Stone Face, had appeared at last. It seems that, many years before, a young man had migrated from the valley and settled at a distant seaport, where, after getting together a little money, he had set up as a shopkeeper. His name—but I could never learn whether it was his real one, or a nickname that had grown out of his habits and success in life—was Gathergold. Being shrewd and active, and endowed by Providence with that inscrutable faculty which develops itself in what the world calls luck, he became an exceedingly rich merchant, and owner of a whole fleet of bulky-bottomed ships. All the countries of the globe appeared to join hands for the mere purpose of adding heap after heap to the mountainous accumulation of this one man's wealth. The cold regions of the north, almost within the gloom and shadow of the Arctic Circle, sent him their tribute in the shape of furs; hot Africa sifted for him the golden sands of her rivers, and gathered up the ivory tusks of her great elephants out of the forests; the East came bringing him the rich shawls, and spices, and teas, and the effulgence of diamonds, and the gleaming purity of large pearls. The ocean, not to be behindhand with the earth, yielded up her mighty whales, that Mr. Gathergold might sell their oil, and make a profit on it. Be the original commodity what it might, it was gold within his grasp. It might be said of him, as of Midas, in the fable, that whatever he touched with his finger immediately glistened, and grew yellow, and was changed at once into sterling metal, or, which suited him still better, into piles of coin. And, when Mr. Gathergold had become so very rich that it would have taken him a hundred years only to count his wealth, he bethought himself of his native valley, and resolved to go back thither, and end his days where he was born. With this purpose in view, he sent a skilful architect to build him such a palace as should be fit for a man of his vast wealth to live in.

As I have said above, it had already been rumored in the valley that Mr. Gathergold had turned out to be the prophetic personage so long and vainly looked for, and that his visage was the perfect and undeniable similitude of the Great Stone Face. People were the more ready to believe that this must needs be the fact when they beheld the splendid edifice that rose, as by enchantment, on the site of his father's old weather beaten farm-house. The exterior was of marble, so dazzlingly white that it seemed as though the whole structure might melt away in the sunshine, like those humbler ones which Mr. Gathergold, in his young play-days, before his fingers were gifted with the touch of transmutation, had been accustomed to build of snow. It had a richly ornamented portico, supported by tall pillars, beneath which was a lofty door, studded with silver knobs, and made of a kind of variegated wood that had been brought from beyond the sea. The windows, from the floor to the ceiling of each stately apartment, were composed, respectively, of but one enormous pane of glass, so transparently pure that it was said to be a finer medium than even the vacant atmosphere. Hardly anybody had been permitted to see the interior of this palace; but it was reported, and with good semblance of truth, to be far more gorgeous than the outside, insomuch that, whatever was iron or brass in other houses was silver or gold in this; and Mr. Gathergold's bedchamber, especially, made such a glittering appearance that no ordinary man would have been able to close his eyes there. But, on the other hand, Mr. Gathergold was now so inured to wealth, that perhaps he could not have closed his eyes, unless where the gleam of it was certain to find its way beneath his eyelids.

In due time, the mansion was finished; next came the upholsterers, with magnificent furniture; then, a whole troop of black and white servants, the harbingers of Mr. Gathergold, who, in his own majestic person, was expected to arrive at sunset. Our friend Ernest, meanwhile, had been deeply stirred by the idea that the great man, the noble man, the man of prophecy, after so many ages of delay, was at length to be made manifest to his native valley. He knew, boy as he was, that there were a thousand ways in which Mr. Gathergold, with his vast wealth, might transform himself into an angel of beneficence, and assume a control over human affairs as wide and benignant as the smile of the Great Stone Face. Full of faith and hope, Ernest doubted not that what the people said was true, and that now he was to behold the living likeness of those wondrous features on the mountain-side. While the boy was still gazing up the valley, and fancying, as he always did, that the Great Stone Face returned his gaze and looked kindly at him, the rumbling of wheels was heard, approaching swiftly along the winding road.

"Here he comes!" cried a group of people who were assembled to witness the arrival. "Here comes the great Mr. Gathergold!"

A carriage, drawn by four horses, dashed round the turn of the road. Within it, thrust partly out of the window, appeared the physiognomy of the old man, with a skin as yellow as if his own Midas-hand had transmuted it. He had a low forehead, small, sharp eyes, puckered about with innumerable wrinkles, and very thin lips, which he made still thinner by pressing them forcibly together.

"The very image of the Great Stone Face!" shouted the people. "Sure enough, the old prophecy is true; and here we have the great man come, at last!"

And, what greatly perplexed Ernest, they seemed actually to believe that here was the likeness which they spoke of. By the roadside there chanced to be an old beggar-woman and two little beggar-children, stragglers from some far-off region, who, as the carriage rolled onward, held out their hands and lifted up their doleful voices, most piteously beseeching charity. A yellow claw—the very same that had clawed together so much wealth—poked itself out of the coach-window, and dropt some copper coins upon the ground; so that, though the great man's name seems to have been Gathergold, he might just as suitably have been nick-named Scattercopper. Still, nevertheless, with an earnest shout, and evidently with as much good faith as ever, the people bellowed,—

"He is the very image of the Great Stone Face!"

But Ernest turned sadly from the wrinkled shrewdness of that sordid visage, and gazed up the valley, where, amid a gathering mist, gilded by the last sunbeams, he could still distinguish those glorious features which had impressed themselves into his soul. Their aspect cheered him. What did the benign lips seem to say?

"He will come! Fear not, Ernest; the man will come!"

The years went on, and Ernest ceased to be a boy. He had grown to be a young man now. He attracted little notice from the other inhabitants of the valley; for they saw nothing remarkable in his way of life, save that, when the labor of the day was over, he still loved to go apart and gaze and meditate upon the Great Stone Face. According to their idea of the matter, it was a folly, indeed, but pardonable, inasmuch as Ernest was industrious, kind, and neighborly, and neglected no duty for the sake of indulging this idle habit. They knew not that the Great Stone Face had become a teacher to him, and that the sentiment which was expressed in it would enlarge the young man's heart, and fill it with wider and deeper sympathies than other hearts. They knew not that thence would come a better wisdom than could be learned from books, and a better life than could be moulded on the defaced example of other human lives. Neither did Ernest know that the thoughts and affections which came to him so naturally, in the fields and at the fireside, and wherever he communed with himself, were of a higher tone than those which all men shared with him. A simple soul,—simple as when his mother first taught him the old prophecy,—he beheld the marvellous features beaming adown the valley, and still wondered that their human counterpart was so long in making his appearance.

By this time poor Mr. Gathergold was dead and buried; and the oddest part of the matter was, that his

Profile, Franconia Notch. Illustration from *White Mountain Scenery* with descriptions by Moses F. Sweetser, a 19th Century Souvenir Book.

wealth, which was the body and spirit of his existence, had disappeared before his death, leaving nothing of him but a living skeleton, covered over with a wrinkled, yellow skin. Since the melting away of his gold, it had been very generally conceded that there was no such striking resemblance, after all, betwixt the ignoble features of the ruined merchant and that majestic face upon the mountain-side. So the people ceased to honor him during his lifetime, and quietly consigned him to forgetfulness after his decease. Once in a while, it is true, his memory was brought up in connection with the magnificent palace which he had built, and which had long ago been turned into a hotel for the accommodation of strangers, multitudes of whom came, every summer, to visit that famous natural curiosity, the Great Stone Face. Thus, Mr. Gathergold being discredited and thrown into the shade, the man of prophecy was yet to come.

It so happened that a native-born son of the valley, many years before, had enlisted as a soldier, and, after a great deal of hard fighting, had now become an illustrious commander. Whatever he may be called in history, he was known in camps and on the battle-field, under the nickname of Old Blood-and-Thunder. This war-worn veteran, being now infirm with age and wounds, and weary of the turmoil of military life, and of the roll of the drum and the clangor of the trumpet, that had so long been ringing in his ears, had lately signified a purpose of returning to his native valley, hoping to find repose where he remembered to have left it. The inhabitants, his neighbors and their grown-up children, were resolved to welcome the renowned warrior with a salute of cannon and a public dinner; and all the more enthusiastically, it being affirmed that now, at last, the likeness of the Great Stone Face had actually appeared. An aid-de-camp of Old Blood-and-Thunder, travelling through the valley, was said to have been struck with the resemblance. Moreover, the school-mates and early acquaintances of the general were ready to testify, on oath, that, to the best of their recollection, the aforesaid general had been exceedingly like the majestic image, even when a boy, only that the idea had never occurred to them at that period. Great, therefore, was the excitement throughout the valley; and many people, who had never once thought of glancing at the Great Stone Face for years before, now spent their time in gazing at it, for the sake of knowing exactly how General Blood-and-Thunder looked.

On the day of the great festival, Ernest, with all the other people of the valley, left their work, and proceeded to the spot where the sylvan banquet was prepared. As he approached, the loud voice of the Rev. Dr. Battleblast was heard, beseeching a blessing on the good things set before them, and on the distinguished friend of peace in whose honor they were assembled. The tables were arranged in a cleared space of the woods, shut in by the surrounding trees, except where a vista opened eastward, and afforded a distant view of the Great Stone Face. Over the general's chair, which was a relic from the home of Washington, there was an arch of verdant boughs, with the laurel profusely intermixed, and surmounted by his country's banner, beneath which he had won his victories. Our friend Ernest raised himself on his tiptoes, in hopes to get a glimpse of the celebrated guest; but there was a mighty crowd about the tables anxious to hear the toasts and speeches, and to catch any word that might fall from the general in reply; and a volunteer company, doing duty as a guard, pricked ruthlessly with their bayonets at any particularly quiet person among the throng. So Ernest, being of an unobtrusive character, was thrust quite into the background, where he could see no more of Old Blood-and-Thunder's physiognomy than if it had been still blazing on the battle-field. To console himself, he turned towards the Great Stone Face, which, like a faithful and long-remembered friend, looked back and smiled upon him trough the vista of the forest. Meantime, however, he could overhear the remarks of various individuals, who were comparing the features the hero with the face on the distant mountain-side.

" 'T is the same face, to a hair!" cried one man, cutting a caper for joy.

"Wonderfully like, that's a fact!" responded another.

"Like! why, I call it Old Blood-and-Thunder himself, in a monstrous looking-glass!" cried a third.

"And why not? He's the greatest man of this or any other age, beyond a doubt."

And then all three of the speakers gave a great shout, which communicated electricity to the crowd, and called forth a roar from a thousand voices, that went reverberating for miles among the mountains, until you might have supposed that the Great Stone Face had poured its thunder-breath into the cry. All these comments, and this vast enthusiasm, served the more to interest our friend; nor did he think of questioning that now, at length, the mountain-visage had found its human counterpart. It is true, Ernest had imagined that this long-looked-for personage would appear in the character of a man of peace, uttering wisdom, and doing good, and making people happy. But, taking an habitual breadth of view, with all his simplicity, he contended that Providence should choose its own method of blessing mankind, and could conceive that this great end might be effected even by a warrior and a bloody sword, should inscrutable wisdom see fit to order matters so.

"The general! the general" was now the cry. "Hush! silence! Old Blood and-Thunder's going to make a speech."

Even so; for, the cloth being removed, the general's health had been drunk, amid shouts of applause, and he now stood upon his feet to thank the company. Ernest saw him. There he was, over the shoulders of the crowd, from the two glittering epaulets and embroidered collar upward, beneath the arch of green boughs with intertwined laurel, and the banner drooping as if to shade his brow! And there, too, visible in the same glance, through the vista of the forest, appeared the Great Stone Face! And was there, indeed, such a resemblance as the crowd had testified? Alas, Ernest could not recognize it! He beheld a war-worn and weather-beaten countenance, full of energy, and expressive of an iron will; but the gentle wisdom, the deep, broad, tender sympathies, were altogether wanting in Old Blood-and-Thunder's visage; and even if the Great Stone Face had assumed his look of stern command, the milder traits would still have tempered it.

"This is not the man of prophecy," sighed Ernest to himself, as he made his way out of the throng. "And must the world wait longer yet?"

The mists had congregated about the distant mountain-side, and there were seen the grand and awful features of the Great Stone Face, awful but benignant, as if a mighty angel were sitting among the hills, and enrobing himself in a cloud-vesture of gold and purple. As he looked, Ernest could hardly believe but that a smile beamed over the whole visage, with a radiance still brightening, although without motion of the lips. It was probably the effect of the western sunshine, melting through the thinly diffused vapors that had swept between him and the object that he gazed at. But—as it always did—the aspect of his marvellous friend made Ernest as hopeful as if he had never hoped in vain.

"Fear not, Ernest," said his heart, even as if the Great Face were whispering him,—"fear not, Ernest; he will come."

More years sped swiftly and tranquilly away. Ernest still dwelt in his native valley, and was now a man of middle age. By imperceptible degrees, he had become known among the people. Now, as heretofore, he labored for his bread, and was the same simple hearted man that he had always been. But he had thought and felt so much, he had given so many of the best hours of his life to unworldly hopes for some great good to mankind, that it seemed as though he had been talking with the angels, and had imbibed a portion of their wisdom unawares. It was visible in the calm and well considered beneficence of his daily life, the quiet stream of which had made a wide green margin all along its course. Not a day passed by, that the world was not the better because this man, humble as he was, had lived.

He never stepped aside from his own path, yet would always reach a blessing to his neighbor. Almost involuntarily, too, he had become a preacher. The pure and high simplicity of his thought, which, as one of its manifestations, took shape in the good deeds that dropped silently from his hand, flowed also forth in speech. He uttered truths that wrought upon and moulded the lives of those who heard him. His auditors, it may be, never suspected that Ernest, their own neighbor and familiar friend, was more than an ordinary man; least of all did Ernest himself suspect it; but, inevitably as the murmur of a rivulet, came thoughts out of his mouth that no other human lips had spoken.

When the people's minds had had a little time to cool, they were ready enough to acknowledge their mistake in imagining a similarity between General Blood-and-Thunder's truculent physiognomy and the benign visage on the mountain-side. But now, again, there were reports and many paragraphs in the newspapers, affirming that the likeness of the Great Stone Face had appeared upon the broad shoulders of a certain eminent statesman. He, like Mr. Gathergold and old Blood-and-Thunder, was a native of the valley, but had left it in his early days, and taken up the trades of law and politics. Instead of the rich man's wealth and the warrior's sword, he had but a tongue, and it was mightier than both together. So wonderfully eloquent was he, that whatever he might choose to say, his auditors had no choice but to believe him; wrong looked like right, and right like wrong; for when it pleased him, he could make a kind of illuminated fog with his mere breath, and obscure the natural daylight with it. His tongue, indeed, was a magic instrument: sometimes it rumbled like the thunder; sometimes it warbled like the sweetest music. It was the blast of war,—the song of peace; and it seemed to have a heart in it, when there was no such matter. In good truth, he was a wondrous man; and when his tongue had acquired him all other imaginable success,—when it had been heard in halls of state, and in the courts of princes and potentates,—after it had made him known all over the world, even as a voice crying from shore to shore,—it finally persuaded his countrymen to select him for the Presidency. Before this time, indeed, as soon as he began to grow celebrated,—his admirers had found out the resemblance between him and the Great Stone Face; and so much were they struck by it, that throughout the country this distinguished gentleman was known by the name of Old Stony Phiz. The phrase was considered as giving a highly favorable aspect to his political prospects; for, as is likewise the case with the Popedom, nobody ever becomes President without taking a name other than his own.

While his friends were doing their best to make him President, Old Stony Phiz, as he was called, set out on a visit to the valley where he was born. Of course, he had no other object than to shake hands with his fellow-citizens, and neither thought nor cared about any effect which his progress through the country might have upon the election. Magnificent preparations were made to receive the illustrious statesman; a cavalcade of horsemen set forth to meet him at the boundary line of the State, and all the people left their business and gathered along the wayside to see him pass. Among these was Ernest. Though more than once disappointed, as we have seen, he had such a hopeful and confiding nature, that he was always ready to believe in whatever seemed beautiful and good. He kept his heart continually open, and thus was sure to catch the blessing from on high when it should come. So now again, as buoyantly as ever, he went forth to behold the likeness of the Great Stone Face.

The cavalcade came prancing along the road, with a great clattering of hoofs and a mighty cloud of dust, which rose up so dense and high that the visage of the mountain-side was completely hidden from Ernest's eyes. All the great men of the neighborhood were there on horseback; militia officers, in uniform; the member of Congress; the sheriff of the county; the editors of newspapers; and many a farmer, too, had mounted his patient steed, with his Sunday coat upon his back. It really was a very brilliant spectacle, especially as there were numerous banners flaunting over the cavalcade, on some of which were gorgeous portraits of the illustrious statesman and the Great Stone Face, smiling familiarly at one another, like two brothers. If the pictures were to be trusted, the mutual resemblance, it must be confessed, was marvellous. We must not forget to mention that there was a band of music, which made the echoes of the mountains ring and reverberate with the loud triumph of its strains; so that airy and soul thrilling melodies broke out among all the heights and hollows, as if every nook of his native valley had found a voice, to welcome the distinguished guest. But the grandest effect was when the far-off mountain precipice flung back the music; for then the Great Stone Face itself seemed to be swelling the triumphant chorus, in acknowledgment that, at length, the man of prophecy was come.

All this while the people were throwing up their hats and shouting, with enthusiasm so contagious that the heart of Ernest kindled up, and he likewise threw up his hat, and shouted, as loudly as the loudest, "Huzza for the great man! Huzza for Old Stony Phiz!" But as yet he had not seen him.

"Here he is, now!" cried those who stood near Ernest. "There! There! Look at Old Stony Phiz and then at the Old Man of the Mountain, and see if they are not as like as two twin brothers!"

In the midst of all this gallant array came an open barouche, drawn by four white horses; and in the barouche, with his massive head uncovered, sat the illustrious statesman, Old Stony Phiz himself.

"Confess it," said one of Ernest's neighbors to him, "the Great Stone Face has met its match at last!"

Now, it must be owned that, at his first glimpse of the countenance which was bowing and smiling from the barouche, Ernest did fancy that there was a resemblance between it and the old familiar face upon the mountain-side. The brow, with its massive depth and loftiness and all the other features, indeed, were boldly and strongly hewn, as if in emulation of a more than heroic, of a Titanic model. But the sublimity and stateliness, the grand expression of a divine sympathy, that illuminated the mountain visage and etherealized its ponderous granite substance into spirit, might here be sought in vain. Something had been originally left out, or had departed. And therefore the marvellously gifted statesman had always a weary gloom in the deep caverns of his eyes, as of a child that has outgrown its playthings or a man of mighty faculties and little aims, whose life, with all its high performances, was vague

The Great Stone Face. Postcard published by Chisholm Bros., Portland, Maine. This is a photograph of Edward Hill's painting *Old Man of the Mountains* which is in the collection of the Littleton (N.H.) Public Library. The postcard is not a photograph of the Profile.

and empty, because no high purpose had endowed it with reality.

Still, Ernest's neighbor was thrusting his elbow into his side, and pressing him for an answer.

"Confess! confess! Is not he the very picture of your Old Man of the Mountain?"

"No!" said Ernest, bluntly, "I see little or no likeness."

"Then so much the worse for the Great Stone

Face!" answered his neighbor; and again he set up a shout for Old Stony Phiz.

But Ernest turned away, melancholy, and almost despondent: for this was the saddest of his disappointments, to behold a man who might have fulfilled the prophecy, and had not willed to do so. Meantime, the cavalcade, the banners, the music, and the barouches swept past him, with the vociferous crowd in the rear, leaving the dust to settle down, and the Great Stone Face to be revealed again, with the grandeur that it had worn for untold centuries.

"Lo, here I am, Ernest!" the benign lips seemed to say. "I have waited longer than thou, and am not yet weary. Fear not; the man will come."

The years hurried onward, treading in their haste on one another's heels. And now they began to bring white hairs, and scatter them over the head of Ernest; they made reverend wrinkles across his forehead, and furrows in his cheeks. He was an aged man. But not in vain had he grown old: more than the white hairs on his head were the sage thoughts in his mind; his wrinkles and furrows were inscriptions that Time had graved, and in which he had written legends of wisdom that had been tested by the tenor of a life. And Ernest had ceased to be obscure. Unsought for, undesired, had come the fame which so many seek, and made him known in the great world, beyond the limits of the valley in which he had dwelt so quietly. College professors, and even the active men of cities, came from far to see and converse with Ernest; for the report had gone abroad that this simple husbandman had ideas unlike those of other men, not gained from books, but of a higher tone,—a tranquil and familiar majesty, as if he had been talking with the angels as his daily friends. Whether it were sage, statesman, or philanthropist, Ernest received these visitors with the gentle sincerity that had characterized him from boyhood, and spoke freely with them of whatever came uppermost, or lay deepest in his heart or their own. While they talked together, his face would kindle, unawares, and shine upon them, as with a mild evening light. Pensive with the fullness of such discourse, his guests took leave and went their way; and passing up the valley, paused to look at the Great Stone Face, imagining that they had seen its likeness in a human countenance, but could not remember where.

While Ernest had been growing up and growing old, a bountiful Providence had granted a new poet to this earth. He, likewise, was a native of the valley, but had spent the greater part of his life at a distance from that romantic region, pouring out his sweet music amid the bustle and din of cities. Often, however, did the mountains which had been familiar to him in his childhood lift their snowy peaks into the clear atmosphere of his poetry. Neither was the Great Stone Face forgotten, for the poet had celebrated it in an ode, which was grand enough to have been uttered by its own majestic lips. This man of genius, we may say, had come down from heaven with wonderful endowments. If he sang of a mountain, the eyes of all mankind beheld a mightier grandeur reposing on its breast, or soaring to its summit, than had before been seen there. If his theme were a lovely lake, a celestial smile had now been thrown over it to gleam forever on its surface. If it were the vast old sea, even the deep immensity of its dread bosom seemed to swell the higher, as if moved by the emotions of the song. Thus the world assumed another and a better aspect from the hour that the poet blessed it with his happy eyes. The Creator had bestowed him, as the last best touch to his own handiwork. Creation was not finished till the poet came to interpret, and so complete it.

The effect was no less high and beautiful, when his human brethren were the subject of his verse. The man or woman, sordid with the common dust of life, who crossed his daily path, and the little child who played in it, were glorified if he beheld them in his mood of poetic faith. He showed the golden links of the great chain that intertwined them with an angelic kindred; he brought out the hidden traits of a celestial birth that made them worthy of such kin. Some, indeed, there were, who thought to show the soundness of their judgment by affirming that all the beauty and dignity of the natural world existed only in the poet's fancy. Let such men speak for themselves, who undoubtedly appear to have been spawned forth by Nature with a contemptuous bitterness; she having plastered them up out of her refuse stuff, after all the swine were made. As respects all things else, the poet's ideal was the truest truth.

The songs of this poet found their way to Ernest. He read them after his customary toil, seated on the bench before his cottage-door, where for such a length of time he had filled his repose with thought, by gazing at the Great Stone Face. And now as he read stanzas that caused the soul to thrill within him, he lifted his eyes to the vast countenance beaming on him so benignantly.

"O majestic friend," he murmured, addressing the Great Stone Face, "is not this man worthy to resemble thee?"

The face seemed to smile, but answered not a word.

***

Now it happened that the poet, though he dwelt so far away, had not only heard of Ernest, but had meditated much upon his character, until he deemed nothing so desirable as to meet this man, whose untaught wisdom walked hand in hand with the noble simplicity of his life. One summer morning, therefore, he took passage by the railroad, and, in the decline of the afternoon, alighted from the cars at no great distance from Ernest's cottage. The great hotel, which had formerly been the palace of Mr. Gathergold, was close at hand, but the poet, with his carpetbag on his arm, inquired at once where Ernest dwelt, and was resolved to be accepted as his guest.

Approaching the door, he there found the good old man, holding a volume in his hand, which alternately he read, and then, with a finger between the leaves, looked lovingly at the Great Stone Face.

"Good evening," said the poet. "Can you give a traveller a night's lodging?"

"Willingly," answered Ernest; and then he added, smiling, "Methinks I never saw the Great Stone Face look so hospitably at a stranger."

The poet sat down on the bench beside him, and he and Ernest talked together. Often had the poet held intercourse with the wittiest and the wisest, but never before with a man like Ernest, whose thoughts and feelings gushed up with such a natural feeling, and who made great truths so familiar by his simple utterance of them. Angels, as had been so often said, seemed to have wrought with him at his labor in the fields; angels seemed to have sat with him by the fireside; and, dwelling with angels as friend with friends, he had imbibed the sublimity of their ideas, and imbued it with the sweet and lowly charm of household words. So thought the poet. And Ernest, on the other hand, was moved and agitated by the living images which the poet flung out of his mind, and which peopled all the air about the cottage-door with shapes of beauty, both gay and pensive. The sympathies of these two men instructed them with a profounder sense than either could have attained alone. Their minds accorded into one strain, and made delightful music which neither of them could have claimed as all his own, nor distinguished his own share from the other's. They led one another, as it were, into a high pavilion of their thoughts, so remote, and hitherto so dim, that they had never entered it before, and so beautiful that they desired to be there always.

As Ernest listened to the poet, he imagined that the Great Stone Face was bending forward to listen too. He gazed earnestly into the poet's glowing eyes.

"Who are you, my strangely gifted guest?" he said.

The poet laid his finger on the volume that Ernest had been reading.

"You have read all these poems," said he. "You know me, then,—for I wrote them."

Again, and still more earnestly than before, Ernest examined the poet's features; then turned towards the

Great Stone Face; then back, with an uncertain aspect, to his guest. But his countenance fell; he shook his head, and sighed.

"Wherefore are you sad?" inquired the poet.

"Because," replied Ernest, "all through life I have awaited the fulfilment of a prophecy; and, when I read these poems, I hoped that it might be fulfilled in you."

"You hoped," answered the poet, faintly smiling, "to find in me the likeness of the Great Stone Face. And you are disappointed, as formerly with Mr. Gathergold, and old Blood-and-Thunder, and Old Stony Phiz. Yes, Ernest, it is my doom. You must add my name to the illustrious three, and record another failure of your hopes. For—in shame and sadness do I speak it, Ernest—I am not worthy to be typified by yonder benign and majestic image."

"And why?" asked Ernest. He pointed to the volume. "Are not those thoughts divine?"

"They have a strain of the Divinity," replied the poet. "You can hear in them the far-off echo of a heavenly song. But my life, dear Ernest, has not corresponded with my thought. I have had grand dreams, but they have been only dreams, because I have lived—and that, too, by my own choice—among poor and mean realities. Sometimes, even—shall I dare to say it? I lack faith in the grandeur, the beauty, and the goodness, which my own works are said to have made more evident in nature and in human life. Why, then, pure seeker of the good and true, shouldst thou hope to find me, in yonder image of the divine?"

The poet spoke sadly, and his eyes were dim with tears. So, likewise, were those of Ernest.

At the hour of sunset, as had long been his frequent

custom, Ernest was to discourse to an assemblage of the neighboring inhabitants in the open air. He and the poet, arm in arm, still talking together as they went along, proceeded to the spot. It was a small nook among the hills, with a gray precipice behind, the stern front of which was relieved by the pleasant foliage of many creeping plants that made a tapestry for the naked rock, by hanging their festoons from all its rugged angles. At a small elevation above the ground, set in a rich framework of verdure, there appeared, a niche, spacious enough to admit a human figure, with freedom for such gestures as spontaneously accompany earnest thought and genuine emotion. Into this natural pulpit Ernest ascended, and threw a look of familiar kindness around upon his audience. They stood, or sat, or reclined upon the grass, as seemed good to each, with the departing sunshine falling obliquely over them, and mingling its subdued cheerfulness with the solemnity of a grove of ancient trees, beneath and amid the boughs of which the golden rays were constrained to pass. In another direction was seen the Great Stone Face, with the same cheer, combined with the same solemnity, in its benignant aspect.

Ernest began to speak, giving to the people of what was in his heart and mind. His words had power, because they accorded with his thoughts; and his thoughts had reality and depth, because they harmonized with the life which he had always lived. It was not mere breath that this preacher uttered; they were the words of life, because a life of good deeds and holy love was melted into them. Pearls, pure and rich, had been dissolved into this precious draught. The poet, as he listened, felt that the being and character of Ernest were a nobler strain of poetry than he had ever written. His eyes glistening with tears, he gazed reverentially at the venerable man, and said within himself that never was there an aspect so worthy of a prophet and a sage as that mild, sweet, thoughtful countenance, with the glory of white hair diffused about it. At a distance, but distinctly to be seen, high up in the golden light of the setting sun, appeared the Great Stone Face, with hoary mists around it, like the white hairs around the brow of Ernest. Its look of grand beneficence seemed to embrace the world.

At that moment, in sympathy with a thought which he was about to utter, the face of Ernest assumed a grandeur of expression, so imbued with benevolence, that the poet, by an irresistible impulse, threw his arms aloft and shouted,—

"Behold! Behold! Ernest is himself the likeness of the Great Stone Face!"

Then all the people looked and saw that what the deep-sighted poet said was true. The prophecy was fulfilled. But Ernest, having finished what he had to say, took the poet's arm, and walked slowly homeward, still hoping that some wiser and better man than himself would by and by appear, bearing a resemblance to the GREAT STONE FACE.

The End

Historical
Epilogue

THE WILLEY SLIDE DISASTER
AND MOUNTAIN CULTURE

Today, just as when *The Ambitious Guest* was published, the most popular mountain literature is about tragedy. Accounts of death and disaster are more popular than stories of determination and success. While there may be a few pleasant stories about successful mountain adventures, there is no doubt that tragedy dominates contemporary mountain writing, for tragedy, the unusual, is news. A successful mountaineering expedition, where all of the participants return home and share their experiences with family and friends is not news. However, when there is an accident, a rescue, and, perhaps most importantly, *death*, then there is news. The 1996 Everest Disaster, where eight climbers died on that mountain, was news then and today continues to be a controversial subject, generating books, television shows, and movies while successful ascents of that same mountain are only memories for those who were there. Similarly, accidents, rescues, and deaths in the White Mountains of New Hampshire become *news* despite the fact that there are many more uneventful family hiking trips, all with very happy endings. The Willey family tragedy was the first natural disaster in American history to capture the attention of the American people. In the years since this disaster there have been other storms and accidents that have claimed more lives in the White Mountains. However, no other storm or incident has had as lasting an impact as this evening thunderstorm that claimed the lives of this pioneering family.

For a story about death to be successful, there must be more than just death. The story must contain real human drama, and it must capture the personality of each victim. Hawthorne accomplishes this in *The Ambitious Guest*. The first readers of this story immediately recognized the incident and family about which it was written since the 1826 Willey family disaster, the deaths of nine people, had received such widespread publicity when it occurred. The story begins:

> One September night a family had gathered round their hearth, and piled it high with the driftwood of mountain streams, the dry cones of the pine, and the splintered ruins of great trees that had come crashing down the precipice. . . This family were situated in the Notch of the White Hills, where the wind was sharp throughout the year, and pitilessly cold in the winter.

Towards the end of the story Hawthorne writes:

> Who has not heard their name? The story has been told far and wide, and will forever be a legend of these mountains. Poets have sung their fate.

Hawthorne underscores the fame of the family by neither naming them nor providing the reader with any specific narration of the true story. The reader of this story must independently recognize that it is a fictionalized account about a real family trapped in a real disaster that costs them their lives. The ensuing publicity and notoriety of the incident brought many people to visit the farm that had been the site of the untimely deaths. Hawthorne and others memorialized a real American family.

This tragedy was important news of the period and much was written about it. Accounts of the storms in the White Mountains and the plight of the Willey family were quickly reported in the newspapers. Perhaps the first account of the disaster was printed in the *New Hampshire Intelligencer* in Haverhill, New Hampshire. The publisher, Sylvester T. Goss, had the opportunity to meet with a "party of gentlemen" from New York who had been in the White Mountains at the time of the storms. On September 9, 1826 the *Boston Courier* printed a long article about the disaster and noted that it was basing its story on the accounts that had appeared in the *New Hampshire Intelligencer*: "As the subject has excited universal sympathy, we believe that an abstract of the account in the Haverhill paper will not be unacceptable to our readers." The "party of gentlemen from New York" must have included the Reverend Carlos Wilcox of Connecticut, whose account of the Willey disaster appeared in the *New York Spectator* on September 15, 1826 and then, on September 19, 1826, in *The New Hampshire Gazette,* published in Portsmouth, New Hampshire.

In a very short period of time the "melancholy details" of the Willey family disaster were known throughout the country and in subsequent years the story would be told and re-told many times. Published in 1833, Grenville Mellen's very long poem *Buried Valley* is about this historical incident but includes very few facts about either Mount Washington or Crawford Notch despite the fact that Mellen had visited the area. The Willey family is described in the "cottage home" and being "cluster'd round it's hearth." Then, "the hills were bow'd into that dreadful vale of slaughter, before the booming water!" and "chaos" becomes their "traceless tomb." In conclusion, Mellen commands of the reader: "Ask not—ask not the tale—Go look upon that BURIED VALE!" Lucy Crawford's *History of the White Mountains,* published in 1846, included a lengthy account of the accident. Benjamin Willey, the Congregational minister in North Conway and brother of Samuel Willey, the victim in the landslide, published *Incidents of White Mountain History* in 1855 and included a lengthy description of White Mountain landslides, in particular the Willey disaster, in his book. Franklin Leavitt, White Mountain guide, map-maker, and poet, included an illustration of the family fleeing from the house on his map of 1854 and later composed a poem about the event. Edward Melcher, one of the members of the rescue party who recovered the victim's bodies from the debris of the landslide, said of the event in 1880: "These terrific scenes which I have attempted to narrate made a deep impression on my memory, and today, at eighty-four years of age, they seem as vivid as on the fated day of their occurrence." In 1902, George Franklyn Willey, a collateral descendent of the victims, published *Soltaire,* a novel which combines a certain mystery of the disaster with a great deal of fantasy and romance. The Reverend Guy Roberts of Whitefield, New Hampshire, published a series of pamphlets about the history of the White Mountains. In his pamphlet about the Willey Slide, published in 1925, he wrote: "The rumble and roar of this great avalanche was heard for miles around reaching as far as Whitefield and other surrounding towns."* F. Allen Burt's *The Story of Mount Washington*, published by Dartmouth College in 1960, includes a lengthy description of the disaster. Eric Purchase's *Out of Nowhere: Disaster and Tourism in the White Mountains*, published in 1999, analyzes the relationship between the Willey disaster and the tourism industry that flourished in the region in the years afterwards.

All of the nineteenth century guide books contained descriptions of the Willey disaster and the family's home. Moses Sweetser noted in his guidebook: "Visitors are escorted through the house on payment of a small fee, but they will see nothing of interest." Samuel Eastman was more explicit when he described the Willey's home: "It has become important as a showplace, twelve and a half cents being charged for showing each person through the house. There is however nothing within the ruinous edifice of sufficient interest to warrant even this trifling expenditure." Stereoscopic pictures of the Willey House were sold as souvenirs to the many tourists who came to the White Mountains in the nineteenth century. Horace Fabyan built a hotel

---

*It is twenty miles from the site of the Willey House to the Town of Whitefield.

adjoining the Willey House in 1845 for the convenience of the many visitors. Chisholm's *White Mountain Guide* of 1880 described the Willey House as "a low and massive old wooden building, to which a rather unpleasant modern structure has been added." Both the hotel and the Willey House were destroyed by fire on September 24, 1899. And today visitors continue to stop and walk around the site, perhaps having some ice cream or taking some pictures, and most certainly wondering why anyone wished to settle in this lonesome spot so long ago.

On the following pages the reader will find different accounts of this White Mountain tragedy and a number of illustrations and photographs of the Willey house and farm. A brief note about the Crawford family may be useful to the reader. Abel Crawford, who was married to Hannah Rosebrook, was the first settler in the isolated valley west of Mt. Washington where he built his cabin in 1791. Eleazar Rosebrook, Crawford's father-in-law, subsequently visited the region and purchased Crawford's farm. Abel Crawford then moved his family further south into the notch where he established another farm and tavern. One of Crawford's sons, Ethan Allen Crawford, born in 1792, married his cousin, Lucy, and they later inherited their Grandfather's farm and tavern. The Crawford family was very important in the settlement of the White Mountains, and in addition to losing crops and animals in the floods of this August 1826 storm, they participated in the search and recovery efforts for the Willey family.

Through the many ways that the Willey family is remembered in literature, paintings, engravings, travel writings, local histories, scientific journals and news-paper articles it is a part of New Hampshire history and folklore. However, and perhaps more importantly, that this story has so endured is testimony to the place that the Willey family has in the history of death and disaster in a larger mountain culture.

Slide at the Willey House. J. D. Whitney from Charles T. Jackson's *Final Report on the Geology and Mineralogy of the State of New Hampshire* published in 1844.

ACCOUNT OF THE LATE SLIDE FROM THE WHITE MOUNTAINS.

IN A LETTER FROM REV. CARLOS WILCOX.

Published in the *New York Spectator* on Friday,
September 15, 1826 and in *The New Hampshire Gazette*
on Tuesday, September 19, 1826

Hanover, (N. H.) 2d Sept. 1826

Dear Sir—I have just returned from an excursion to the White Mountains, and shall now spend a day of rest in this village, in giving you some account of the effects produced by the most destructive fall of rain ever known in that region. It happened on the night of the 28th of August which will be long remembered in this part of the country.

I left Hanover on Saturday last, in company with two gentlemen of my acquaintance from the city of New York, and rode as far as Haverhill, where we all spent the Sabbath. The road over which we passed was like a bed of ashes two or three inches deep; and the country around us exhibited the usual effects of a long drought. The abundant rains that fell three weeks ago, over the Southern half of New England, did not reach the upper part of the valley of Connecticut River. On Monday morning it began to rain in Haverhill, and continued along our route for most of the day, but so moderately and at such intervals, that with the help of great coats and umbrellas we proceeded on our journey in an open waggon as far as Bethlehem, fifteen miles west of the White Mountains. As we approached the vicinity of the Mountains, the rain increased till it became a storm, and compelled us to stop about the middle of the afternoon.

The storm continued most of the night; but the next morning was clear and serene. The view from the hill of Bethlehem was extensive and delightful. In the Eastern horizon Mount Washington, with the neighboring peaks on the North and on the South, formed a grand outline far up in the blue sky. Two or three small fleecy clouds rested on its side, a little below its summit, while from behind this highest point of land in the United States East of the Mississippi, the sun rolled up rejoicing in his strength and glory. We started off toward the object of our journey with spirits greatly exhilerated by the beauty and grandeur of our prospect.

As we hastened forward with our eyes fixed on the tops of the mountains before us, little did we think of the scene of destruction around their base, on which the sun was now for the first time beginning to shine. In about half an hour we entered Bretton Woods, an unincorporated tract of land covered with a primitive forest, extending on our road five miles to Rosebrook's Inn, and thence six miles to Crawford's, the establishment begun by Rosebrook's father, as described in the travels of Dr. Dwight. On entering this wilderness we were struck with its universal stillness. From every leaf in its immense masses of foliage the rain hung in large glittering drops; and the silver note of a single unseen and unknown bird was the only sound that we could hear.

After we had proceeded a mile or two the roaring of the Amonoosuck began to break in upon the stillness and soon grew so loud as to excite our surprise. In consequence of coming to the river almost at right angles, and by a very narrow road, through trees and bushes very thick, we had no view of the water, till with a quick trot we had advanced upon the bridge too far to recede, when the sight that opened at once to the right and to the left, drew from all of us similar exclamations of astonishment and terror; and we hurried over the trembling fabrick as fast as possible.

After finding ourselves safe on the other side, we walked down to the brink; and, though familiar with mountain scenery, we all confessed that we had never seen a mountain torrent before. The water was as thick with earth as it could be, without being changed into mud. A man living near in a log hut showed us how it was at day-break. Though it had fallen six feet, he assured us that it was still ten feet above its ordinary level. To this add its ordinary depth of three or four feet, and here at day-break was a body of water twenty feet deep, and sixty feet wide, moving with the rapidity of a gale of wind between steep banks covered with hemlocks and pines, and over a bed of large rocks, breaking its surface into billows like those of the ocean.

After gazing a few moments on this sublime sight, we proceeded on our way, for the most part of some distance from the river, till we came to the farm of Rosebrook, lying on its banks. We found his fields covered with water, and sand, and flood wood. His fences and bridges were all swept away; and the road was so blocked up with logs, that we had to wait for the labors of men and oxen, before we could get to his house. Here we were told that the river was never before known to bring down any considerable quantity of earth, and were pointed to bare spots on the sides of the White Mountains, never seen till that morning. As our road, for the remaining six miles, lay quite near the river and crossed many small tributary streams, we employed a man to accompany us with an axe. We were frequently obliged to remove trees from the road, to fill excavations, to mend and make bridges, or contrive to get our horses and waggon along separately. After toiling in this manner for half a day we reached the end of our journey, not however without being obliged to leave our waggon half a mile behind. In many places, in these six miles, the road and the whole adjacent woods, as it appeared from the marks on the trees had been overflowed to the depth of ten feet. In one place the river, in consequence of some obstruction at a re-markable fall, had been twenty feet higher than it was when we passed.

We stopped to view the fall, which Dr. Dwight calls "beautiful." He says of it—"The descent is from fifty to sixty feet, cut through a mass of stratified granite; the sides of which appear as if they had been laid by a mason in a variety of fantastical forms; betraying, how-ever, by their rude and wild aspect, the masterly hand of nature." This description is sufficiently correct; but the beauty of the fall was now lost in its sublimity. You have only to imagine the whole body of the Amonoosuck, as it appeared at the bridge which we crossed, now compressed to half its width, and sent downward at an angle of 20 or 25 degrees, between perpendicular walls of stone.

On our arrival at Crawford's the appearance of his farm was like that of Rosebrook's, only much worse. Some of his sheep and cattle were lost; and eight hun-dred bushels of oats were destroyed. Here we found five gentlemen, who gave us an interesting account of

The Willey House. William H. Bartlett for *American Scenery*, London 1838.

their unsuccessful attempt to ascend Mount Washington the preceding day. They went to the "Camp" at the foot of the mountain on Sabbath evening, and lodged there with the intention of climbing the summit the next morning. But in the morning the mountains were enveloped in thick clouds; and the rain began to fall, and increased till afternoon, when it came down in torrents. At five o'clock they proposed to spend another night at the camp and let the guide return home for a fresh supply of provisions for the next day. But the impossibility of keeping a fire where everything was so wet, and at length the advice of their guide, made them all conclude to return, though with great reluctance. No time was now to be lost, for they had seven miles to travel on foot, and six of them by a rugged path through a gloomy forest. They ran as fast as their circumstances would permit; but the dark evergreens around them and the black clouds above, made it night before they had gone half the way. The rain poured down faster every moment; and the little streams, which they had stepped across the evening before, must now be crossed by wading, or by cutting down trees for bridges, to which they were obliged to cling for life. In this way they reached the bridge over the Amonoosuck near Crawford's just in time to pass it before it was carried down the current.

On Wednesday, the weather being clear and beautiful, the waters having subsided, six gentlemen with a guide went to Mount Washington, and one accompanied Mr. Crawford to the "Notch," from which nothing had yet been heard. We met again at evening, and related to each other what we had seen. The party who went to the Mountain were five hours in reaching the site of the camp, instead of three, the usual time. The path for nearly one third of the distance was so much excavated, or covered with miry sand, or blocked up with flood wood, that they were obliged to grope their way through thickets almost impenetrable, where one generation of trees after another had risen and fallen, and were now lying across each other in every direction, and in various stages of decay. The Camp itself had been wholly swept away; and the bed of the rivulet, by which it had stood, was now more than ten rods wide, and with banks from ten to fifteen feet high. Four or five other brooks were passed, whose beds were enlarged, some of them to twice the extent of this. In several the water was now only three or four feet wide, while the bed of ten, fifteen, or twenty rods in width, was covered for miles with stones from two to five feet in diameter, that had been rolled down the mountains, and through the forests, by thousands, beating everything before them. Not a tree, nor the root of a tree, remained in their path. Immense piles of hemlocks and other trees, with their limbs and barks entirely bruised off, were lodged all the way on both sides, as they had been driven in among the standing and half standing trees on the banks. While the party were climbing the Mountain, thirty slides were counted, some of which began near the line where the soil and vegetation terminate, and growing wider as they descended, were estimated to contain more than a hundred acres. These were all on the western side of the mountains. They were composed of the whole surface of the earth, with all its growth of woods, and its loose rocks, to the depth of 15, 20, and 30 feet. And wherever the slides of two projecting mountains met, forming a vast ravine, the depth was still greater.

Such was the report which the party from the mountains gave. The intelligence which Mr. Crawford, and the gentleman accompanying him, brought from the Notch, was of a more melancholy nature. The road, though a turnpike, was in such a state, that they were obliged to walk to the Notch House, lately kept by Mr. Willey, a distance of six miles. All the bridges over the Amonoosuck, five in number, those over the Saco, and those over the tributary streams of both, were gone. In some places the road was excavated to the depth of 15 or 20 feet; and in others it was covered with earth, and rocks, and trees, to as great a height. In the Notch, and along the deep defile below it, for a mile and a half, to the Notch House, and as far as could be seen beyond it, no appearance of the road, except in one place for two or three rods, could be discovered. The steep sides of the mountains, first on one hand and then on the other, and then on both, had slid down into this narrow passage, and formed a continued mass from one end to the other, so that a turnpike will probably not be made through it again very soon if ever.

The Notch House was found uninjured; though the barn adjoining it by a shed was crushed; and under its ruins were two dead horses. The house was entirely deserted; the beds were tumbled, their covering was turned down; and near them upon chairs and on the floor lay the wearing apparel of the several members of the family; while the money and papers of Mr. Willey were lying in his open bar. From these circumstances it

Avalanches in the White Mountains, lithograph after a sketch by Daniel Wadsworth, from Theodore Dwight's *Sketches of Scenery and Manners in the United States*, New York, 1829. This was one of the earliest published illustrations of the landslides in the White Mountains after the Willey family disaster of 1826. Note the figure on the rock (foreground lower right) looking across the valley at the landslides on the far mountains.

seemed almost certain, that the whole family were destroyed; and it soon became quite so, by the arrival of a brother of Mr. Crawford from his father's six miles further East. From him we learnt that the valley of the Saco for many miles, presented an uninterrupted scene of desolation. The two Crawfords were the nearest neighbours of Willey. Two days had now elapsed since the storm, and nothing had been heard of his family in either direction.—There was no longer any room to doubt, that they had been alarmed by the noise of the destruction around them, had sprung from their beds, and fled naked from the house, and in the utter darkness had been soon overtaken by the falling mountains and rushing torrents. The family, which is said to have been amiable and respectable, consisted of nine persons, Mr. Willey and his wife and five young children of theirs, with a hired man and boy. After the fall of a single slide last June, they were more ready to take the alarm, though they did not consider their situation dangerous as none had ever been known to fall there previous to this.

Whether more rain fell now than had ever been known to fall before in the same length of time, at least since the sides of the mountains were covered with so heavy a growth of woods, or whether the slides were produced by the falling of such a quantity of rain so suddenly, after the earth had been rendered light and loose by the long drought, I am utterly unable to say. All I know is, that at the close of a rainy day, the clouds seemed all to come together over the White Mountains, and at midnight discharge their contents at once, in a

The Willey Slide, woodcut illustration for John Farmer, *A Catechism of the History of New Hampshire*, 1829. The woodcut shows people fleeing from the house as rocks fall towards it.

terrible burst of rain, which produced the effects that have now been described. Why these effects were produced now, and never before, is known only to Him, who can rend the heavens when he will, and come down, and cause the mountains to flow down at his presence.

Yours, &c.
Carlos Wilcox

Notch of the White Mountains and the Willey House. Published on the cover of *Rural Repository*, Hudson, New York. August 10, 1844.

RURAL REPOSITORY
A SEMI-MONTHLY JOURNAL, EMBELLISHED WITH ENGRAVINGS

Hudson, N. Y.
Saturday, August 10, 1844
Volume XX. Number 26

The above engraving presents a view of the Notch house and its appendages as they now appear. The buildings—even the barn more recently erected—are fast falling into decay: the doors are spread open and off of the hinges—the windows are broken, and the rain descends through the roof from the defective shingles. The material of the whole house are falling away and are as perishable and evanescent as the thousand names which, since the catastrophe of 1826, have been carved or written upon the walls and wainscoting...

...As no one lived to relate the story, no one can tell what occurred on that fateful night, in the interesting family at the Notch house. The slide which came upon the house was in depth from twenty to twenty-five feet, and had expanded, bringing down a prodigious mass of trees, rocks and earth, confusedly mixed together, to the width of some twelve or fifteen rods. Singular as it may appear, this immense body, when it arrived within the distance of not more than two rods of the house, struck a rock of sufficient size and depth to cause a separation of the moving mass, the one portion passing off on the lower end, over the road about forty rods to the south, and the other overwhelming and destroying the barn at no very great distance from the house...

The Willey House, stereoscopic by Benjamin W. Kilburn of Littleton, New Hampshire. Photograph shows the hotel that was built there in 1845 by Horace Fabyan. The hotel and the Willey house were destroyed by a fire on September 24,1899.

HISTORY OF THE
WHITE MOUNTAINS*
LUCY CRAWFORD - 1846

August 26th, there came a party from the west to ascend the mountain, but as the wind had been blowing from the south for several days, I advised them not to go that afternoon, but they said their time was limited and they must proceed. Everything necessary for the expedition being put in readiness, we all, like so many good soldiers, with our staves in our hands, set forward at six o'clock and arrived at the camp at ten o'clock; and I with my knife and flint struck fire, which caught in a piece of dry punk, which I carried for that purpose, and from that I could make a large fire. As this was the only way we had in those days of obtaining fire, and after my performing the duties of a cook and house maid, we sat down in the humble situation of Indians, not having the convenience of chairs, and told stories till the time for rest. The wind still continuing to blow from the south.

In the morning, about four o'clock, it commenced raining, which prevented their hopes of ascending the mountain that day, and not having provisions for another day, and they being unwilling now to give it up,

---

*First published in 1846, Lucy Crawford's *History of the White Mountains* is one of the most important books ever published about the White Mountains. The authorship of the book might be more accurately described as "by Ethan Allen Crawford as told to Lucy, his wife." In her book we find a narrative of the settlement of the White Mountains which describes the activities of the Crawford family and their neighbors. Reprinted here is Lucy Crawford's description of the disaster that befell the Willey family in 1826.

The Willey House. From *Gems of American Scenery Consisting of Stereoscopic Views Among the White Mountains* by Albert Bierstadt and Edward Bierstadt, New York, 1878. Photograph probably taken around 1860.

when they had got so near, a meeting was called and it was unanimously agreed that I should go home and get new supplies and then return to them again. I obeyed their commands; shouldered my empty pack, took my leave of them and then returned; but, as the rain was falling so fast, and the mud collected about my feet, my progress was slow and wearisome. I at length got home, and being tired and my brother Thomas being there, I desired him to take my place, which he cheerfully consented to do, and in a short time, he was laden and set forward, and when arriving at the camp, the party was holding a council as to what was to be done, for the rain had fallen so fast and steadily that it had entirely extinguished the fire. They consulted Thomas upon the matter to know if they had time to get in. He told them to remain there would be very unpleasant, as they must suffer with the wet and cold, not considering danger, but if they would go as fast as they could, they might reach the house; each taking a little refreshment in his hands, and having the precaution to take the axe with them, set off in full speed, and when they came to a swollen stream, which they could not ford, Thomas would, with his axe, fall a tree, for a bridge, and then they would walk over. They got along tolerably well until they came to a large branch, which came from the Notch, this was full and raging, and they had some difficulty to find a tree that would reach to the opposite bank, but at length succeeded in finding one, and they all got safely over, and those who could not walk, crawled along, holding on by the limbs, and when they came to the main stream, the water had risen and come into the road for several rods, and when they crossed the bridge it trembled under their feet. They all arrived in safety about eight o'clock in the evening, when they were welcomed by two large fires to dry themselves. Here they took off their wet garments, and those that had not a change of their own, put on mine and went to bed, while we set up to dry theirs. At eleven o'clock we had a clearing up shower, and it seemed as though the windows of heaven were opened and the rain came down almost in streams; it did not, however, last long before it all cleared away and became a perfect calm.

The next morning we were awakened by our little boy coming into the room, and saying, "Father, the

earth is nearly covered with water, and the hogs are
swimming for life." I arose immediately and went to
their rescue. I waded into the water and pulled away
the fence, and they swam to land. What a sight! The
sun rose clear; not a cloud nor a vapor was to be seen;
all was still and silent, excepting the rushing sound of
the water, as it poured down the hills! The whole
intervale was covered with water a distance to be seen,
of over two hundred acres of land, when standing on
the little hill which has been named and called Giant's
Grave, just back of the stable, where the house used to
stand that was burnt. After standing here a short time,
I saw the fog arise in different places on the water, and
it formed a beautiful sight. The bridge, which had so
lately been crossed, had come down and taken with it
ninety feet of shed which was attached to the barn that
escaped the fire in 1818. Fourteen sheep that were under it were drowned, and those which escaped looked
as though they had been washed in a mud puddle. The
water came within eighteen inches of the door in the
house and a strong current was running between the
house and stable. It came up under the shed and underneath the new stable, and carried away timber and
wood—passed by the west corner of the house and
moved a wagon which stood in its course.

Now the safety of my father and of the Willey family
occupied our minds—but there was no way to find out
their situation. At or near the middle of the day (Tuesday), there came a traveller on foot who was desirous
of going down the Notch that night, as he said his business
was urgent, and he must if possible, go through. I told
him to be patient, as the water was then falling fast, and
as soon as it should fall and I could swim a horse, I would

carry him over the river. Owing to the narrowness of the intervales between the mountains here, when it begins to fall, it soon drains away. At four o'clock I mounted a large strong horse, took the traveller on behind, and swam the river, and landed him safely on the other side and returned. He made the best of his way down to the Notch house and arrived there just before dark. He found the house deserted of every living creature, excepting the faithful dog, and he was unwilling at first to admit the stranger. He at length became friendly and acquainted. On going to the barn he found it had been touched by an avalanche and fallen in. The two horses that were in it were both killed, and the oxen confined under the broken timber tied in their stalls. These he set at liberty after finding an axe and cutting away the timber: they were lame but soon got over it. What must have been the feelings of this lonely traveller while occupying this deserted house—finding doors opened and bed and clothes as though they had been left in a hurry, bible open and laying on the table as it seemed it had lately been read. He went round the house, and prepared for himself a supper, and partook of it alone, except the company of the dog, who seemed hungry like himself—then quietly laid down in one of these open deserted beds and consoled himself by thinking the family had made their escape and gone down to my father's.

Early the next morning he proceeded on his way and he had some difficulty in getting across some places, as the earth and water were mixed together and made a complete quagmire. He succeeded in getting to father's, but could obtain no information of the unfortunate family. He told this story as he went down through Bartlett and Conway, and the news soon spread.

On Wednesday the waters had subsided so much that we could ford the Amanoosuc River with a horse and wagon, and some of the time-limited party agreed to try the ground over again; and they, with the addition of another small party who came from the West on Tuesday, and Thomas for guide, again set out, while I, with a gentleman from Connecticut, went towards the Notch. After travelling a distance of two miles in a wagon, we were obliged to leave it and take to our feet. We now found the road in some places entirely demolished, and seemingly, on a level surface; a crossway which had been laid down for many years and firmly covered with dirt—that to the eye of human reason it would be impossible to move—taken up, and every log had been disturbed and laid in different directions. On going still a little farther, we found a gulf in the middle of the road, in some places ten feet deep, and twenty rods in length. The rest of the road—my pen would fail should I attempt to describe it—suffice it to say, I could hardly believe my own eyes, the water having made such destruction. Now, when within a short distance of the house, found the cows with their bags filled with milk, and from their appearance, they had not been milked for some days. My heart sickened as I thought what had happened to the inmates of the house. We went in and there found no living person—and the house in the situation just described. I was going down to my father's to seek them out, but the gentleman with me would not let me go, for he said he could not find his way back alone, and I must return with him. We set out and arrived home at four o'clock in the afternoon.

I could not be satisfied about the absent family, and again returned, and when I got back to the house found a number of the neighbors had assembled and no information concerning them could be obtained, and my feelings were such that I could not remain there during the night, although a younger brother of mine, being one of the company, almost laid violent hands upon me to compel me to stay, fearing some accident might befall me, as I should have to feel my way through the Notch on my hands and knees, for the water had in the narrowest place in the Notch taken out the rocks which had been beat in from the ledge above, to make the road, and carried them into the gulf below, and made a hole or gulf twenty feet deep, and it was difficult, if not dangerous, to get through in the night—as all those who visited this scene of desolation will bear testimony to; but my mind was fixed and unchangeable, and I would not be prevailed on to stay.

I started and groped my way home in the dark, where I arrived at ten o'clock in the evening. Here I found that the party from the mountain had arrived; as they had nowhere to stay, they were obliged to come in that night. Now we began to relate our discoveries. They had much difficulty in finding their way, as the water had made as bad work with their path as it had done with the road, in proportion to its length. The water had risen and carried away every particle of the camp and all my furniture there. The party seemed thankful that they, on Monday, had made their escape. What must have been their fortune had they remained there? They must have shared the same fate the Willey family did, or suffered a great deal with fear, wet, cold, and hunger, for it would have been impossible for them to have come in until Wednesday, and their provisions must have been all gone, if not lost, on Monday night.

The Willey place before the slide. Woodblock drawn by Marshall M. Tidd.

It seemed really a Providential thing in their being saved. No part of the iron chest was ever found, or anything it contained, excepting a few pieces of blanket that were caught on bushes in different places down the river.

The next morning our friends, with gratitude, left us; and we had the same grateful feelings towards them, wishing each other good luck.

The same day (Thursday) before I had time to look about me and learn the situation of my farm, and estimate the loss I had sustained, the friends of the Willey family had come up to the deserted house and sent for me. At first I said I could not go down, but being advised to, I went. When I got there, on seeing the friends of that well-beloved family, and having been acquainted with them for many years, my heart was full and my tongue refused utterance, and I could not for a considerable length of time speak to one of them, and could

The Willey place after the slide. Woodblock drawn by Marshall M. Tidd. Lucy Crawford prepared, but never published, a revised edition of her *History of the White Mountains*, first published in 1846. Tidd's illustrations were prepared for the revised edition to depict feats and events that are recounted in the book.

only express my regards I had to them in pressing their hands—but gave full vent to tears. This was the second time my eyes were wet with tears since grown to manhood. The other time was when my family was in that destitute situation. Diligent search being made for them, and no traces to be found until night, the attention of the people was attracted by the flies, as they were passing and repassing underneath a large pile of floodwood. They now began to haul away the rubbish, and at length, found Mr. and Mrs. Willey, Mr. Allen, the hired man, and the youngest child, not far distant from each other. These were taken up, broken and mangled, as must naturally be expected, and were placed in coffins; and the next day they were interred, on a piece of ground near the house, and there to remain until winter. Saturday, the other hired man was found and interred; and on Sunday, the eldest daughter was found, some way from where the others were, across the river; and it was said her countenance was fair and pleasant; not a bruise or a mark was discovered upon her. It was supposed she was drowned. She had only a handkerchief around her waist—supposed for the purpose of having someone to lead her by. This girl was not far from twelve years of age. She had acquired a good education, considering her advantages, and she seemed more like a gentleman's daughter, of fashion and affluence, than the daughter of one who had located himself in the midst of the mountains. It is said the earliest flowers are the soonest plucked, and this seemed to be the case with this young, interesting family; the rest of the children were not inferior to the eldest, considering their age.

In this singular act of Providence, there were nine taken from time into eternity—four adult persons and five children. It should remind us, we who are living, to "be also ready, for in such an hour as ye think not, the Son of Man cometh." It was a providential thing, said Zara Cutler, Esq., who was present afterwards, that the house itself was saved, so near came the overwhelming avalanche. The length of the slides are several miles down the side of the mountain. The other three children, one a daughter and the other two sons, have never to this day been found; not even a bone has ever been picked up or discovered. It is supposed they must have been buried deep, underneath an avalanche.

Mr. and Mrs. Willey sustained good and respectable characters, and were in good standing among the Christians in Conway, where they belonged. They were remarkable for their charities and kindness towards others, and commanded the respect of travellers and all who knew them. Much more could be said in their favor, but it would be superfluous to add. Suffice it to remark that the whole intention of their lives was to live humbly, walk uprightly, deal justly with all, speak evil of none.

There came a large slide down back of the house in a direction to take the house with it, and when within ten or fifteen rods of the house it came against a solid ledge of rock and here stopped and separated, one on either side of the house, taking the stable on one side, and the family on the other—or they might have got to the rendezvous; but there is no certainty which of these divisions overtook them, as they were buried partly by the three slides which had come together eighty rods from the house; the two that separated back of the house here met, and a still larger one had come down in the place where Mr. Willey had hunted out a refuge for safety. When the slide was coming down and separating, it had great quantities of timber with it; one log, six feet long and two feet through, still kept its course and came within three feet of the house; but fortunately it was stopped by coming against a brick, where it rested; the ends of trees were torn up, and looked similar to an old peeled birch broom.—The whole valley, which was once covered with beautiful green grass, was now a complete quagmire, exhibiting nothing but ruins of the mountains, heaps of timber, large rocks, sand and gravel. All was dismal and desolate. For a monument, I wrote with a piece of red chalk on a planed board this inscription:

The Family found here.

I nailed it to a dead tree, which was standing near the place where they were found; but it has since been taken away by some of the occupants of the house and used for fuel.

But to return to my own affairs at home:—Fences mostly gone—farm in some places covered so deeply with sand and gravel that it was ruined; and, on the intervale, was piled in great and immense quantities, floodwood, in different places all over it. The bridge now lay in pieces all around the meadow, and the shed also; there was a large field of oats, just ready to harvest, from which I think I would have had four or six hundred bushels—these were destroyed; and some hay in the field was destroyed.—My actual loss at this time was more than one thousand dollars; and truly things looked rather unfavorable. After the fire, we had worked hard and economized closely to live and pay our former dues, which we made slow progress in; as it was necessary for the benefit of the public, I had to buy so many things, which we could not get along without, I could do but little towards taking up my old notes, but still I must persevere, and keep doing while the day lasted; and I thought no man would be punished for being unfortunate. Therefore, taking these things into consideration, I would still continue to do the best I could and trust the event. My father suffered still more than myself. The best part of his farm was entirely destroyed. A new saw mill which he had just put up, and a great number of logs and boards, were swept away together into the sand; fences on the intervale were all gone; twenty-eight sheep were drowned, and considerable grain which was in the field was swept away. The water rose on the outside of the house twenty-two inches, and ran through the whole house on the lower floors and swept out the coals and

The Notch of the White Mountains with the Willey House. Plate #3, by Isaac Sprague, from William Oakes' *Scenery of the White Mountains*, Boston, 1848.

ashes from the fireplace. They had lighted candles which were placed in the windows, and my mother took down a pole which she used as a clothes pole, and stood at a window near the corner of the house, and would push away the timber and other stuff that came down against the house, when the current run swift, to keep it from collecting in a great body, as she thought it might jam up and sweep away the house; for the water was rising fast. And while thus engaged, she was distressed by the cries of the poor bleating and drowning sheep that would pass by in the flood and seemed to cry for help, but none could be afforded.

My father at this time was from home, and but few of the family were there, so they made the best they could of it. This came on so suddenly and unexpected that almost everything in the cellar was ruined, and a part of the wall fell in.

This loss of my father's property, which he had accumulated only by the sweat of his brow, was so great that he will never be likely to regain it. Many suffered more or less who lived on this wild and uncultivated stream, as far as Saco.

We had now a difficulty which seemed almost insurmountable. The road in many places was entirely gone; the bridges, the whole length of the turnpike excepting two, a distance of seventeen miles, gone; the directors came and looked at it, and found it would take a large sum to repair it. The good people of Portland, however, to encourage us, raised fifteen hundred dollars to help us with; it was put into the hands of Nathan Kinsman, Esq., to see it well laid out. The directors voted to raise an assessment on the shares to make up the balance; and that, with some other assistance, was divided into jobs and let out, and we all went to work; and, as it was said, the sun shone so short a time in this Notch, that the hardy New Hampshire boys made up their hours by moonlight.

Willey House, Stereoscopic No. 87. Photographed and published by Kilburn Brothers of Littleton, New Hampshire.

WHITE MOUNTAIN SCENERY
WITH DESCRIPTIONS BY M. F. SWEETSER
Published by Chisholm Brothers, Portland, Maine, 1879.

From the Preface

The object of this volume is to afford to visitors among the WHITE MOUNTAINS a *souvenir* of their grand scenery, as well as to enable those who have not yet seen them to obtain an idea of their exceeding majesty and beauty. ... In one respect at least, and that an important one, the pictures herein contained are superior to any other collection of illustrations of the WHITE MOUN-TAINS. They are in no way idealized or exaggerated, as is customary in such works, but present faithful tran-scripts of the actual scenes as painted by the sun. The impressions were made with lithographic ink, and are as permanent as the letter press; so that the fidelity of a photograph is secured without its perishability. It is also hoped that the descriptions appended to the pictures may be of some value, as showing the localities of the various scenes and their relations to other points among the highlands.

From Sweetser's description:

THE OLD WILLEY HOUSE—
White Mountain Notch

Three miles south of the Crawford House, in the nar-row pass between Mount Willey and Mount Webster, stands this famous little building. It was erected in 1793 to serve as a public house for travelers on the old Coos road; and many years later was occupied by Samuel

The old Willey House, White Mountain Notch. White Mountain Scenery with descriptions by M. F. Sweetser. Chisholm Brothers, Portland, Maine, 1879

Willey, Jr., and his family. On the night of the 28th of August, 1826, after a long drought, a deluge of rain broke over the adjacent peaks, and detached an avalanche of rocks, earth, and trees from the parched sides of Mount Willey, just back of and over the house. The family rushed out in terror, and were swept away and killed in the terrible downward rush of the land-slide. The bodies of Mr. and Mrs. Willey and two children and two hired men were found amid the chaos of rocks, broken and mutilated. The remains of the other three children were never recovered. If they had remained in the house, all would have been saved, as the avalanche struck a tall rock back of the building and was separated into two streams, which flowed on either side of the house, leaving it altogether unharmed. A modern inn has been built alongside, where a few summer boarders sojourn. The white buildings are visible from the railway for a long distance, as the trains traverse the White Mountain Notch.

THE WILLEY HOUSE
A BALLAD OF THE WHITE HILLS
by Dr. Thomas William Parsons[*]

You see that cottage in the glen,
   You desolate forsaken shed—
Whose mouldering threshold, now and then,
   Only a few stray travellers tread.

No smoke is curling from its roof,
   At eve no cattle gather round,
No neighbor now, with dint of hoof,
   Prints his glad visit on the ground.

A happy home it was of yore;
   At morn the flocks went nibbling by,
And Farmer Willey, at his door,
   Oft made their reckoning with his eye.

Right fond and pleasant, in their ways,
   The gentle Willey people were;
I knew them in those peaceful days,
   And Mary—every one knew her.

Two summers now had seared the hills,
   Two years of little rain or dew;
High up the courses of the rills
   The wild rose and the raspberry grew;

---

[*]In 1855 *Putnam's Magazine* published Dr. Parsons' ballad about the Willey family tragedy. It was reprinted in full in Thomas Starr King's *The White Hills*, published in 1871. Excerpts from the poem are reprinted here.

The mountain sides were cracked and dry,
   And frequent fissures on the plain,
Like mouths, gaped open to the sky,
   As though the parched earth prayed for rain.

One sultry August afternoon,
   Old Willey, looking toward the West,
Said—"We shall hear the thunder soon;
   Oh! if it bring us rain, 'tis blest."

And even with his word, a smell
   Of sprinkled fields passed through the air
And from a single cloud there fell
   A few large drops—the rain was there.

Ere set of sun a thunder-stroke
   Gave signal to the floods to rise;
Then the great seal of heaven was broke!
   Then burst the gates that barred the skies!

While from the west the clouds rolled on,
   And from the nor'west gathered fast;
"We'll have enough of rain anon,"
   Said Willey—"if this deluge last."

For soon they went to their repose,
   And in their beds, all safe and warm,
Saw not how fast the waters rose,
   Heard not the growing of the storm.

But just before the stroke of ten,
   Old Willey looked into the night,
And called upon his two hired men,
   And woke his wife, who struck a light,

Though her hand trembled, as she heard
 The horses whinnying in the stall,
And—"children!" was the only word,
 That woman from her lips let fall.

"Mother!" the frighted infants cried,
 "What is it? has a whirlwind come?"
Wildly the weeping mother eyed
 Each little darling, but was dumb.

For down the mountain's crumbling side,
 Full half the mountain from on high
Came sinking, like the snows that slide
 From the great Alps about July.

Willey House, White Mountains. Stereoscopic picture, unknown photographer. Note the bare rocks, the scars from the landslide, behind the Willey House and the hotel.

And with it went the lordly ash,
　　And with it went the kingly pine,
Cedar and oak amid the crash,
　　Dropped down like clippings of the vine.

At morn the men of Conway felt
　　Some dreadful thing had chanced that night,
And some by Breton woods who dwelt
　　Observed the mountain's altered height.

Old Crawford and the Fabyan land
　　Came down from Amonoosuc then,
And passed the Notch—ah! strange and sad
　　It was to see the ravaged glen.

But having toiled for miles, in doubt,
　　With many a risk of limb and neck,
They saw, and hailed with joyful shout,
　　The Willey House amid the wreck.

And in the dwelling—O despair!
　　The silent room! the vacant bed!
The children's little shoes were there—
　　But whither were the children fled?

That day a woman's head, all gashed,
　　Its long hair streaming in the flow,
Went o'er the dam, and then was dashed
　　Among the whirlpools down below.

And when the Willey House is gone,
　　And its last rafter is decayed,
Its history may yet live on
　　In this your ballad that I made.

THE WILLEY SLIDE
FRANKLIN LEAVITT*

Eighteen hundred and twenty-six
  The Willey Mountain down did slip;
It missed the house and took the barn,
  If they'd all staid in they'd met no harm

It being in the dark of night
  The Willey family took a fright,
And out of the house they all did run
  And on to them the mountain come.

It buried them all up so deep
  They did not find them for three weeks,
And three of them were never found
  They were buried there so deep in the ground.

*Franklin Leavitt (1824-1900?), of Lancaster, New Hampshire, and his son, Victor, published a series of maps of the White Mountains between 1852 and 1888 which were sold as souvenirs. The maps included very simple folk art telling the history of the White Mountains. Later in his life Leavitt took to putting some of the local history into verse. Illustration: *The Willey Family Fleeing their house*, from Leavitt's *Map of the White Mountains, 1854.*

HARPER'S MONTHLY MAGAZINE[*]

JUNE 1881

Volume LXIII Number CCCLXXIII

We descended to the houses at the mountain's foot by this still plain path. One and the other are associated with the most tragic event connected with the history of the great Notch.

Since quite early in the century, the smaller house, the walls of which were scribbled over by curious pilgrims, was kept as an inn, and for a long time it was the only stopping place between Abel Crawford's below and Captain Rosebrook's above, a distance of thirteen miles. Its situation at the entrance to the Notch was advantageous to the public, but attended with a danger which seems not to have been sufficiently regarded, if, indeed, it caused successive inmates particular concern. This fatal security had a lamentable sequel.

In 1826 this house was occupied by Samuel Willey, his wife, five children, and two hired men. During the summer a drought of unusual severity dried the streams and parched the thin soil of the mountains. On the 28th of August, at dusk, a storm burst upon the mountains, and raged with indescribable fury throughout the night. The rain fell in sheets. Innumerable torrents suddenly broke forth on all sides, deluging the narrow valley, and bearing with them forests that had covered the

---

[*]In 1881 *Harper's Monthly* published a series of three articles by Samuel Adams Drake about the White Mountains. Drake's book, *The Heart of the White Mountains: Their Legend and Scenery*, was published in 1882.

mountains for ages. The turbid and swollen Saco rose over its banks, flooding the intervales, and spreading destruction in its course.

Two days afterward a traveller succeeded in forcing his way through the Notch. He found the Willey house standing uninjured in the midst of woful desolation. A land-slide descending from Mount Willey had buried the little vale beneath its ruins. The traveller reported at the nearest house what he had seen. Assistance was dispatched to the scene of disaster. The rescuers came too late to render aid to the living, but they found, and buried on the spot, the bodies of Mr. and Mrs. Willey and the two hired men. The children were never found.

The Willey House, White Mts., N.H. Souvenir stereoscopic card by N. W. Pease of North Conway, N. H.

SOLTAIRE

A ROMANCE OF THE WILLEY SLIDE AND THE WHITE MOUNTAINS

byGeorge Franklyn Willey[*]
New Hampshire Publishing Corporation
Manchester, New Hampshire 1902

WHY WRITTEN.

The writer of the following story has been from childhood familiar with the White Mountain region. Born
within a half-score miles, as the crow flies, of the tragic
"Willey slide," and bearing the same name as the family so suddenly eliminated, familiar with the legends
of the event, and with the conjectures of the "oldest
inhabitants" as to the fate of those who were never
found, he has taken the time from his other occupa-
tions to put into this romance something both of
tradition and conjecture. The Author.

CHAPTER I
IN THE PATH OF THE AVALANCHE

"An everlasting hill was torn
From its primeval base, and borne,
In gold and crimson vapors dressed,
To where a people are at rest.
Slowly it came in its mountain wrath,

---

[*]A review in *The Granite Monthly* described Willey's book as an
"historical novel." The review continued: "It is most emphatically a
New Hampshire book, as its theme, scenes, plots, and incidents are
all within the state, woven together by one native to the state, printed
in Concord and published in Manchester... The story of the anni-
hilation of the Willey family by the hurling down of that mass of
matter from Mount Willard (Willey) is one that has always had a
singular interest from the time of its occurrence to the present, and
will have as long as the White Mountains shall endure."

And the forests vanished before its path.
And the rude cliffs bowed, and the waters fled,
And the living were buried, while over their head
They heard the full march of their foe as he sped,
And the valley of life was the tomb of the dead."

Crawford's Notch is a term to suggest at once to the mind of the tourist a double significance, the nobility and grandeur of man and the grandeur and nobility of the mountains. Those who remember the Patriarch of the Hills, for whom this wild gorge was named, recall a specimen of rugged virility, an ideal mountaineer. A puny form and weakened intellect might pass among the masses without creating any surprise, but a dwarfed physique is not looked for in the wild domains of Nature. Neither do we look for any ordinary architecture in the mighty formation of these monarchs of New England's mountains, lifting their snow-crowned crests—

"Like earth's gigantic sentinels
Discoursing in the skies."

Thirty miles in length from the narrow opening at Fabyan's to the broad outlet of Conway's meadows, for nearly two miles eastward and downward from Crawford's, the Notch is scarcely more than a fissure between two masses of huge rock—a defile twenty-two feet in width overhung by rocky ramparts from twelve to twenty feet in height—looking as if the giant powers of earth had risen in their might and moved back the mountains so that the river, finding its life current in the crystal fountains of the White Hills, might make its escape to the intervales below.

Furniture Belonging to the Willey Family. Stereo by Clough & Kimball, photographers, Concord, N. H. circa 1870.

As the valley continues it grows wider, though the retreating mountains, Mount Willey on the one side and Mount Webster on the other, lift their heads to the height of over three thousand feet. Down the rock-ribbed sides of these giants leap clear streams, feeders of the wild Saco. One of these tributaries affords the Silver Cascade, a display of waterfalls no tourist fails to visit. There is also the Flume, possessing a weird, lonely grandeur, while farther down is that stream of more melancholy interest known as "Nancy's Brook." At once the sad story of the deserted maid seeking her recreant lover is recalled, and the sympathetic comer drops a tear over the unhappy fate of the poor girl who perished here of hunger and cold, when she could no longer continue her search for him. Perhaps a little of the sting of her sorrow is removed by the realization that he suffered for what he made her endure, for the spirit of "an eye for an eye and a tooth for a tooth" still lives in the human breast.

If we look upon the river in the cheer-less songs of its rushing waters as lacking sentiment, the dusky hunter, whose snowy canoe first skimmed its foaming current, claimed that it was more divine than human, having sprung from the tears of the Great Manitou in his grief over a fallen people. But the scenery, rather than the conceptions of a race we could never understand, attracts us. From the rugged splendor of the granite gateway to the peace and good cheer of the quiet vales it is impossible to find landscapes more beautiful or sublime. Overhung by the luxuriant foliage of majestic trees lining either bank, the Saco, soon after leaving the Gate, rolls on in a more subdued manner when in its peaceful moods, through its natural archway of green. But between the river and the elements there is sometimes war; and then beware!

Crawford's Notch was first seen by a white man, a hunter named Nash, from a treetop on Cherry Mountain, in 1772, only three years before the first battle of the Revolution. Until then the scattered settlers above and around the White Hills had been obliged to travel to the lower settlements by circuitous routes around the mountains. So the discovery of this passway was hailed with pleasure, and the hardy pioneers were soon trying its difficult and dangerous course.

The passage, however, proved so toilsome and perilous that as early as 1793 a road was laid out from Conway to the town of Coös, and that year a sort of half-way house was built by a man named Davis under the overhanging cliffs of one of the mountains. This dwelling, on account of the tragical fate of a family at one time occupying it, became known as "the Willey House." A little grassy meadow stretched along the river bank in front of the place, and though the mountain came so near on the other side that a great rock reared its massive front almost over its roof, the surroundings of this isolated home suggested peace and repose. The occasional wayfarer, braving the hardships of the lonely pass either on business or pleasure, had reason to bless the sturdy settler who made his humble home the haven of comfort to the pilgrim.

Increased travel called for a better road, and in 1803 this route was incorporated as the tenth turnpike in the state. Immediately streams of traffic passing to and fro between that region and Portland, as well as travelers following where fortune led them, showed the need of this enterprise by greatly increased numbers. In winter it was no uncommon sight to see the winding valley road dotted for a mile at a stretch by teams from the north country laded with pork, cheese, butter, and lard. The horses were tough Canadian animals, able to withstand the rigor of the severe climate, while their drivers were tall, stout men of giant frames and sinews of iron, who urged their panting steeds on through the blinding storms of snow and sleet, or cutting blasts of cold, with loud shouts and bluster which awoke the mountain solitude far and wide.

Henry Hill then lived at this house, while six or seven miles below him was a tavern kept by that patriarch of the Mountains, Abel Crawford, and where the White Mountain House stands was the Roseberry hostelry. Later Mr. Hill moved away and the Davis house remained empty until, in the summer of 1825, Captain Samuel Willey and his family went there to live. At this time Ethan Crawford lived at the Glen, while his father had removed to the upper end of the Notch, near the site of the present Crawford House.

Kept by stalwart men, who were as prompt to brave the perils that beset the storm-driven wayfarers of the American Alps as the monks of St. Bernard were to battle for the poor wanderers of the Swiss winterland, these old-time hostelries, could their history be written, would afford an interesting chapter in New England pioneer life.

Here, the day's arduous journey done, the tired horses fed and made as comfortable as possible for the long, cold night, the wayfarers having eaten to their fill of the plain but nutritious fare of the times, washed down with generous draughts of old Medford rum, circled about the fireplaces heaped high with blazing logs, smoked their corn-cob pipes and exchanged the gossip of the day, or if there was nothing of more recent development to hold their attention, narrated anew the thrilling deeds of days not yet grown gray, of bloody scenes in Indian warfare still fresh in memory, or retold the story of that closing act in the great drama of the French and Indian wars, the last retreat of the rangers of the North, or the tale of Lovewell's dearly bought victory of the plains of the Saco.

The Willeys were genial, hospitable people, and they soon made themselves loved and respected by the travelers who stopped with them during the year which followed. Nothing unusual occurred to break the even tenor of their lives until another June, when they witnessed a scene which made a lasting impression on their minds.

One of those landslides which have left their last-ing traces on the mountain-sides, like the tracks of some mighty road builder, the reddish or yellowish hue of the barren pathway contrasting vividly with the deep green of the forests, then plunged from the dizzy cliffs overhead into the valley below, leaving a desolate path behind and a mound of ruin where it fell. These slides or avalanches of earth generally break from their con-nection with the steep ascent near the border of the scrub vegetation where the layer of earth is thin and its hold on the rocks slight. Narrow and shallow at first the avalanche widens and deepens as it moves down-ward, gaining fresh impetus as it advances, until a broad belt of loose earth and boulders is swept on, bearing with its great areas of forest, with a thunderous noise and shaking the mountain to its very foundation.

It was such a sight as this that Captain Willey and his wife saw one misty June afternoon, but the avalanche passed beyond them without doing any harm. Still, it had so awakened the fears of Captain Willey, that pres-ently he took the precaution to build a place of refuge a short distance from his house to which they could flee in case another avalanche should threaten them.

A severe drought set in, so that by the last of Au-gust the mountain region seemed crisped to a powder. The dust lay in the road ankle deep, and everywhere vegetation was parched and lifeless. On Sunday, the 25th, a rainstorm broke the dry spell, and steadily in-creased in violence until on Monday night it had reached unprecedented fury and volume. Between nine o'clock that evening and the following dawn the Saco rose twenty-four feet, and its angry, swollen waters swept the valley from the Notch to the intervales of Conway with ruin and desolation.

With the experienced eye of a mountaineer, Captain Willey had noticed at sunset the black and ominous appearance of the heavens, which were belted with column on column of storm-clouds moving slowly and grandly across the western sky in the direction of the north, covering Mount Washington with fold upon fold of the darkest drapery.

With a feeling of gladness that the drought was over, and without dreaming of what was to take place before another morning, the doomed family retired at half-past ten, though not to sleep. At least the parents remained awake, though it may be some of the five children fell into the innocent slumber of childhood.

At eleven a distant rumbling was heard above the sullen roar of the river, rapidly increasing in volume and depth until the deep muttering grew into a hoarse thunder. Understanding what the solemn warning meant, Captain Willey cried,—

"Hark, Polly! it is coming. There is not mistaking that sound. Quick—the children—the refuge—before it is too late."

Mrs. Willey was already beside the children trying to rouse them for the flight from the house, which it was felt was in the direct course of the oncoming slide.

Two men employed by Captain Willey rushed into the room, for the noise was now so loud and ominous as to arouse the deepest sleeper. The rain had ceased, and a few straggling stars were to be seen as the little group of frightened people reached the doorway. The towering mountain trembled from pinnacle to base under the mighty power assailing it, and the cottage home under its frowning heights rocked like a cradle.

The better to protect themselves in their place of refuge the men seized bedding to bear to the retreat, while Mrs. Willey undertook to guide the children there. Eliza, the oldest, was but twelve, an exceedingly bright and attractive girl, while there were Jeremiah, aged eleven, Martha, aged nine, Elbridge, seven, and Sally, in her mother's arms, only three. Elbridge clung to his older sister, and the rest kept beside their mother.

The roar of the maddened river was deafening, but the thunder rolling down from the mountain behind them was more terrifying. No pen has yet written the horror of that situation; imagination is not vivid enough to portray it.

> "Beware the pine tree's withered branch
> Beware the awful avalanche!"

In that dreadful flight Martha slipped and fell. Her mother was trying to find her when the awful storm reached the little party. The feeble cries of the ill-fated family were lost in the grinding of rocks upon rocks, the descent of forests upon billows of earth, the crash, the shock, the reverberation. Past the chosen spot of death and desolation the runaway river swept on to more peaceful scenes, while overhead the pale stars increased in numbers, and the moon struggled into sight, the cheerless watcher of a cheerless night.*

---

*In the remaining seven chapters the author contrives an incredible story of fantasy and romance. To begin with, Martha Willey is rescued from the disaster of that August night by a mysterious hermit named Soltaire, a recluse because he was unable to marry the girl of his choice. After rescuing Martha the hermit takes her to a remote cave on Black Mountain in Jackson, New Hampshire, and the story continues from there. —Editor

A FINAL RESTING PLACE

"To the memory of the family which was at once destroyed by a slide from the White Mountains on the night of 28 August 1826."

—Gravemarker at the Willey family cemetery, Intervale, New Hampshire. Though their names are listed on the headstone, the bodies of Jeremiah, Martha, and Sally have never been found.

Samuel Willey, Jr.	March 31, 1788
Polly Lovejoy Willey	April 19, 1791
Eliza Anne Willey	July 19, 1814
Jeremiah L. Willey	July 30, 1815
Martha Glazier Willey	September 22, 1816
Elbridge Gerry Willey	July 13, 1819
Sally Willey	July 11, 1823

The hired farm workers killed in the landslide: David Allen, born around 1789, was buried in Bartlett, New Hampshire. The gravesite of David Nickerson, born around 1805, is unknown.